Able Gate

By

Douglas Hirt

Wolfpack Publishing
P.O. Box 620427
Las Vegas, NV 89162

Print Edition ISBN: 978-1-62918-732-7

Able Gate

By

Douglas Hirt

1

I HAD NEVER SEEN Barrister McClain until that day he rode past the plate-glass window of the Money Jar Cafe, scowling into a low eastern sun, reining to a stop in the middle of the street.

His face was ugly enough to melt a mud fence. Cur dogs cowarded out of his path and brave men suddenly found themselves interested in the mundane store window displays. He rode a stump-broke mare and carried a converted Remington .44 in a cross-draw rig on his left hip.

"Gate! Able Gate," he called with his face screwed up and looking like it had stopped a Sioux war club. "I know you're around. Show yourself."

From behind me came a startled cry. Mary Landers had been bringing the coffeepot across the crowded floor and now she, like everyone else in the cafe, was staring out the window at the black-coated apparition astride a gray horse.

"I'm waiting for you, Gate. You can't hide from me, you know that. I'll track you to hell and back if I have to," he said. Then, as if a whirlwind had blown through town, the doorways all along the street sucked the sidewalks clean of women and children. The men lingered a moment longer, but when I looked again the street was empty as church on Monday morning.

Mary's wide brown eyes glanced questioningly at me and her mouth parted as if an anchor had attached itself to her chin. "You?" she more mouthed than spoke.

"Me?" I replied, surprised. "My name is Gatelatch, remember? Not Able Gate! It is certainly not me he is looking for," I said. I hoped I had impressed her with my indignation at the very thought.

She let go of a breath. "Well, I didn't think so, at least I hoped not. Who is Able Gate, and who is that man?"

I glanced out the window at whom she was pointing and pushed the spectacles up the bridge of my nose. Barrister McClain turned in his saddle with a stare that would ignite dry tinder and surveyed the empty street. He was the nastiest of the sordid McClain clan—a family up over the border. They're descendants of an Irish mountain man and a Blackfoot woman and nowadays they work a small parcel of land, but rumor has it more than a few head of Montana beef hang salted in their smokehouse. Prudently, no one has examined the rumor too closely. If the devil had kin on this earth, then the McClains were them, and if he had a blood brother, Barrister was it.

Mary was watching me expectantly. Her lovely brown eyes and smooth skin were both the gift of youth and good breeding. Slender as a willow with all the bends in the right places, she wore a white apron over a blue dress. At twenty-five and not yet married, she was something of a conversation piece and a prize to be won. I also was something of a conversation piece, but no one had shown much interest in winning me, and that was probably just as well.

"His name is Barrister McClain," I said. She needed no further explanations. "McClain? What is he doing here?"

I shrugged and held up my empty cup to remind Mary of the steaming pot of coffee in her hand. "He's the family gun shark. Not that they aren't all good with a gun, but Barrister is the best of them, and he enjoys killing," I said. "I suspect he is looking for the man who killed his brother, Ryan, about four months ago up around Billings."

Her concerned eyes moved from me to the window and then back again. "Able Gate is that man?"

"Uh-huh. That's what I hear."

Her eyes narrowed. "How do you know that?"

I shrugged it off and said, "There was some talk about it around the post a few months back."

Mary seemed to shiver and glanced back out the window at Barrister McClain. He had dismounted and was walking his horse across the street to the Custer Saloon. He looped the reins around the hitching rail. The saloon was not open this early in the morning, but that didn't stop his shoulder from bursting the door in. Randy Linger would be hanging a GONE FISHING sign in his window about now, I mused.

"Who is this man that he's looking for, Able Gate?"

"Just another man with a fast gun," I said, sipping the fresh coffee.

"Well," she said with a finality that indicated she had made up her mind on the matter of Barrister McClain and Able Gate, "I certainly hope he doesn't find Gate here."

"So do I," I said truthfully. "So do I."

I finished my breakfast, paid Mary at the front door, and received an unexpected but quite delightful smile in return. A high point, I suspected, in what might turn out to be a very bad day. On the sidewalk outside I glanced across the street and let my view linger a moment on the open door of the saloon. Barrister McClain had a reputation that stretched a bloody line from the Canadian border down to the mining camps of Colorado. He was feared as far west as Utah where he had been known to travel occasionally to express his disapproval of the Mormons there—usually with a gun, but he was big enough and powerful enough that he could express himself just fine with his fists. He didn't move east very often. The law was steadily growing more intolerant from that direction and there was the cavalry, too, both strong deterrents to Barrister McClain. That was why I never expected him to show up here, not with Fort Evan Woods only a mile out of town.

The shops along the street were slowly unburdening themselves of their sudden inflow of folks. I suspected the shopkeepers had managed to capitalize on McClain's sudden arrival—at least it had been good for someone other than the local undertaker.

I put McClain out of mind and turned toward home. The sun was high enough above the horizon now to bring a strong, early morning brilliance to the green leaves of the trees in the park. Their color leaped out with hidden life normally lost from view for the rest of the hot, hazy day. In the sky, soft clouds banked one after the other and rounded to a horizon of a slightly paler blue. I started down the street thinking about the complications involved in catching that subtle shift of color on canvas. It was far more pleasant than thinking about the man in the Custer Saloon. I glanced diagonally across the street and noted with mild amusement that the passersbys there were giving the open door a wide berth.

The house I live in is the last one on A Street. Beyond it the town peters out to tall, rolling Montana grass. I slowed my pace and stopped behind an ancient cottonwood tree that had stood at the corner of Main and A Street long before there had been a Main and A, or clapboard homes to break up the gentle lines of rolling hills.

I tried not to be obvious, but it is difficult to peek around an immense tree trunk without looking suspicious. Tippi Mullroy's front yard was deserted; a wave of relief swept over me as I stepped out and quickened my pace. Passing her front door, I noted the absence of several red roses that had been blooming on the bush by her gate this morning when I had left for breakfast. I made it safely past her yard and was striding up to my front door when…

"Oh, Mr. Gatelatch." A flour-colored face beamed out at me from her opened door, gray hair tied into a bun at the back of her head. I had never seen her wear it any other way.

I stopped with my hand upon the doorknob. Caught a moment too soon. "Good morning, Tippi," I said pleasantly, wishing I had been half a minute quicker. But it wouldn't have made any difference. Tippi Mullroy had been lying in ambush for me behind the curtains of her front window.

Tippi stepped out onto her front porch and we met by the low wrought-iron fence that encompassed her yard, separating it from mine. "It's such a lovely morning, isn't it, Mr. Gatelatch?"

She always insisted on formality when speaking with me, even though she had made it clear early on that I should simply call her Tippi. Mrs. Mullroy made her sound like an old lady, she thought.

"Yes, it is," I agreed briefly, not wanting to be dragged into the conversation that I knew was coming.

"You are up early," she said.

"I went out to breakfast."

Tippi's pale-blue eyes widened. "Oh? Then you saw Mary?"

She came straight on with the frontal attack I had half expected and should have been better at avoiding. Tippi Mullroy had enlisted all the "nice girls" in town into her army of virgins, and she was bound and determined to get me to re-up with one of them.

"Yes, I saw Mary," I said.

"Mary is such a nice girl," Tippi said with feeling.

"I suppose," I said, anxious to get inside. But I could see no way to break free short of a blunt good-bye, and Tippi was too sweet a lady to do that to, so I stood there looking for an avenue of retreat. But I preferred not to allow Tippi to drag me into a discussion about all the "nice girls" in town.

I nodded at the rose bush by her gate and said, "You picked them this morning."

"Oh, you noticed them. Weren't they lovely, Mr. Gatelatch? I so love red roses. You know, the first flower the Sergeant gave me was a yellow desert rose. Well, it wasn't really a rose, only the flower of a prickly pear cactus, but it was lovely just the same."

I knew that, and I knew all about their courtship down in Arizona before John Mullroy joined the cavalry, but I smiled and listened as she told the story again. When she finished I saw a breach in her advance, and I said I ought to be getting to work.

"I baked cookies last night," she countered immediately, and I knew what that meant. She had snuck in a secret rear attack.

Resigned, I hefted a leg over the black iron fence and followed Tippi into the house. It was a house almost identical to the one I lived in, which wasn't surprising considering we both paid rent to the same landlord, the United States Government. It was cheap rent.

Where my house was cluttered and poorly furnished and laid about with canvases, easels, and paints, Tippi's home was neat and tidy. It was cluttered too, only her clutter was perfectly organized, each item a story and a memory.

She let the door hang open as we went inside and the morning sunlight streaming through fell upon the faded roses of an embroidered sofa. It reminded me of Tippi: faded now, but reminiscent of a rich and colorful past, yet still sturdy with a lot of good years left in both of them.

"Now you just wait here one minute, Mr. Gatelatch," she said, waving a hand at the tightly packed furniture. I slid between a low table that banged against my shin and sat down upon a curved loveseat upholstered in the same faded material as the sofa. Tippi hurried across a rose-colored threadbare carpet and through a doorway I knew opened onto a dining room.

I took a deep breath and told myself to be patient. Letting it out slowly, I leaned back into the loveseat hoping they wouldn't be oatmeal cookies again.

All around me were arranged her memories. A canary cage hung in one corner. The happy bird the Sergeant had surprised her with on her birthday had died long ago. The cage was now home to a potted flower with violet petals. A buffet against one wall contained the dishes she and the Sergeant had purchased after their wedding and had carefully moved around the West from one post to the next. Upon a small table by the window stood four kachina dolls she laughingly referred to as her children. She had adopted them while on a tour of duty down in New Mexico. The Sergeant and Tippi had once had a child of their own. The little girl had died in an Indian raid 20 years ago, at least that is what they told themselves. Sara Ann's body was never found.

The mantel above the fireplace held a clock, two green plants, a pinecone from the redwoods the Sergeant had brought back one year from California, and a seashell too. There was a modern tinplate of Sara Ann at five years old riding a child's rocking horse, and an older daguerreotype of Tippi and the Sergeant on their wedding day. He hadn't been in the army then, he joined later, and he was a much older man when I met him back in '76 when we came across the high plains together with the Seventh Cavalry. I had been a young illustrator assigned to make a pictorial record of Custer's Indian campaigns; by that time John Mullroy had been an experienced Indian fighter.

Above the mantel hung a painting I had titled "Reno's Defense." I had painted it a year ago from sketches I had made twelve years earlier, huddled in a hole and leaping back and forth between pencil and Springfield as we held a line against the Sioux while three miles to the north a rising dust cloud marked Custer's final battle. I didn't get to record that scene until almost three days later. The first sergeant in the painting had not been John Mullroy, but when Tippi saw it tears flooded her eyes and she said that it was the Sergeant, right down to the war lance scar on his cheek. I hadn't painted a scar but Tippi wanted one to be there so she saw it. Well, I made her a present of it and lied a little when I told her I'd been at John Mullroy's side when a Sioux arrow cut him down. It seemed to comfort her even after all these years.

Tippi came back into the parlor and set a tin of cookies on the low table next to a vase of freshly cut roses.

"Some nice oatmeal cookies for you, Mr. Gatelatch," she said, sitting in a cane rocking chair across from me.

"Thank you." I tried to sound pleased. It's not that I disliked oatmeal cookies—it's just that Tippi kept slipping them my way faster than I could eat them.

A moment of silence closed in around us and I thought I saw a chance to escape back to the comfort of my own clutter when Tippi said all at once, "I spoke to Mary Landers yesterday. Mary is such a nice girl."

We had come full circle.

"Are you going to the dance at the armory next Saturday night?" she asked.

"I don't know," I said, coming forward in the seat.

Tippi winked at me. "Perhaps I shouldn't be telling you this," she said, glancing about, "but I am certain if you were to ask Mary to the dance she would be delighted to accompany you, Mr. Gatelatch."

"Is that what you two talked about yesterday, Tippi?"

Her pale cheeks pinkened and suddenly I knew why Mary had bestowed that unexpectedly warm parting smile on me as I had left the cafe. What had Tippi told Mary? Perhaps that I was eager to escort her to the armory dance Saturday night?

Now I knew it was time to leave. "Thank you," I said, standing, "I will remember that. Well, I really must be going. I've work to do before I lose the morning light."

She smiled understandingly. Artists, after all, are peculiar people requiring just the right light and just the right mood to work in, and if I could keep her believing that, I had at least one weapon in my arsenal to use to make decorous departures and avoid Saturday night socials at the armory.

I went to the door, her oatmeal cookies in hand, and she waved as I stepped back over the fence. I shut my door behind me and made room for the tin of cookies on a table that was already overflowing.

All my art supplies are packed together for easy transport in a wooden case made especially for me by an appreciative captain down in southern Texas. I had painted a portrait of his wife and daughter, and had helped him out in other ways too.

The case was forty-two inches long, twenty inches high, and eight inches deep. It was a beautiful thing constructed by Mexican craftsmen of polished mesquite and gold-plated brass fittings. Opened, it held all my colors, solvents, brushes, palettes, rags, and something else too. Lifting out the inner panel revealed a standard issue .45-55 Springfield carbine and a standard issue .45 Colt army revolver that had had the barrel changed to four and three-quarter inches. My holster and some ammunition all fitted neatly inside.

I checked the guns then replaced the false panel. I put an easel and canvas under my arm and started for the door. Then I stopped, seeing my reflection in the hall mirror.

In the straight-cut hunting jacket and tan pants I looked every bit the artist Mr. Abernathy B. Gatelatch was supposed to be. The wire-rimmed spectacles added a convincing touch, I thought, tugging a floppy cloth hat on my head. No one would ever see Able Gate behind the garb of an inoffensive artist. At least I hoped not—not with Barrister McClain roaming the streets.

Able Gate

2

TWO MILES OUT OF TOWN, I turned the rented buggy off the road and up a wooded draw that followed the twisting course of a stream back into a stand of trees. I set the brake and paused to survey the quiet summer morning. Water whispered softly to my left while the leaves overhead remained motionless in the still, hot air. In the open areas heat was rising off the ground, carrying with it the pungent odor of grass mixed with the heavier fragrance of pine and poplar.

It was the sort of day on which a man could lie back and enjoy watching clouds if he hadn't anything better to do. A nothing-could-go-wrong sort of day.

I tossed off my jacket and unpacked the "art supplies," strapping the Colt revolver to my hip and rolling up my shirtsleeves. The horse seemed content to remain where he was, munching the tall grass, so I left him there and carried the Springfield with me a few hundred yards farther up the draw.

Back among the trees an ancient chuck-wagon skillet hung from a thick leather strap tied up over a branch. It was rusted and battered and its thick iron edges were chipped and gouged. Its rusty red color was mottled with lead-gray splatters and its heavy bottom was puckered and dented to the point where, upon close examination, I was not able to find one flat surface left on it.

The leather thong was wearing thin; frayed and chinked where more than a few fliers had taken their toll, but sound enough for today. I glanced around the nearby trees to confirm my privacy and slapped a voracious mosquito that had attacked my left forearm.

Twenty yards back was an area that someday might be mined for its brass content. At the moment the deposits lay about the trampled grass in the form of spent .45 cartridges. I loosened the gun in its holster and eyed the skillet swaying gently back and forth by the leather.

"Son," I recalled my father saying on a steaming summer day in Kansas as he lazed out of the sun, leaning back in a chair beneath the shade of an overhead balcony. "It's not how fast you clear the leather that counts, it's how straight the bullet flies." I might have been twelve or thirteen at the time, and I don't remember what had brought up the subject, but those words stuck with me and more than once have borne out true.

The gun slipped smoothly from its holster, tipped up at my waist in an easy movement that felt right in every way. I paused half a second to allow my brain to join in on what my eyes and hands were doing, then the hammer fell, the gun leaped in my fist, and that old skillet went twirling away at the end of its leather thong.

I glanced across the clearing at the horse. He was looking curiously back at me, but not unduly distressed by the gunfire, and shortly returned to the more serious business at hand of munching grass.

I holstered the gun and tried again. The skillet was still swinging widely from my first shot when the second bullet sent it spinning back in a sweeping arc.

The horse didn't bother to look up this time.

It was my father who had taught me to shoot at skillets. They were stout, durable targets you didn't have to keep setting up when your bullet knocked them over. I recalled him taking me out back behind the house and together we'd make that old pan that mother had allowed us to use, once he had agreed to buy her a new one, dance at the end of a rusty chain nailed to the branch of a mulberry tree.

I was eight years old when he first put his huge cap-and-ball revolver in my hands and pointed me at an empty nail keg he'd set up not very far away. He held my little hands in his great big hands, and when the gun roared and bucked and that wooden keg splintered apart, he clapped me proudly on the back. He had carried that old-fashioned gun through the war and remained in close company with it throughout his adult life, shunning the convenience of metallic cartridges for the familiarity of the well-worn 1860 Army Colt.

"I prefer to load my own, son," he said once, later in life when I had aged some and thought I knew better than he. "I know how this old gun prefers to shoot. We've grown old together; I've no need for another."

I tipped the gun out of my holster and squeezed the trigger. The bullet went high and smashed into the skillet's handle, sending it seesawing out of the way. Well, my father had been right about that too. After years of carrying the same gun your hand just sort of grows to fit the grips. It feels right. The same was true for a rifle. There were better and faster rifles to be had these days, but none of them seem to fit my shoulder and lay in my hands as easily as the '73 Springfield carbine that I'd carried for the last dozen years. I suppose part of the reason is that it was designed for a cavalry man: a man between five feet six inches and five feet eight, and no more than one hundred fifty pounds. I slotted right into the upper range of those numbers—officers were given some leeway when it came to height and weight—and the Springfield fit as naturally to me as the shirt on my back.

"When you find something that works well for you, son, stick with it."

He lived by that motto.

I snapped off two more shots that sent the skillet spinning away in a dizzy circle and thought how often you don't realize how smart your parents really were until you have grown up to be as old as they were.

Growing up, all I ever wanted to be was a lawman like he was. But it was he who had urged me to go back East to art school. He had been wise enough to see something in me I couldn't. I discovered I did have a talent for framing the real world on canvas. And I might still be back in New York City, putting frames around bits and pieces of life, had not my father taken a load of buckshot in the back one cold, drizzling night.

At the funeral I made the vow that was expected of a son and went after his killers. All my father's training came back to me as if I had never left his side. They had been four, and they had been as mean as yellow jackets, and I killed each in his turn…like shooting skillets dangling from chains.

Afterward, I knew I could never return to the East and the school. I had changed in those few moments when a man looks into the eyes of another man whose blood is draining away into the dust. That sudden sharp pang hits you like a bullet between your shoulder blades. You've just killed a man! Never mind that he deserved killing…

The skillet had slowed to a gentle sway as I ejected the five spent shells, added them to the growing deposit of brass at my feet, and replaced them with five fresh shells from the Union Metallic Cartridge Company box I had brought along. I lowered the hammer on an empty chamber and holstered the piece.

Moving back a hundred fifty yards to another future brass mine, I did some work with the Springfield, feeling the reassuringly solid thump of it against my shoulder each time I squeezed the trigger. Afterward I put some more rounds through the pistol. It was nearing one o'clock when I packed the weapons back into the case and drove the buggy back to town.

I dropped the rental off at the livery stable by the edge of town and filled my arms with easel and canvas and case and walked home.

Private Frederick Lundt was dozing upon the seat of Colonel Oliver Rundles's carriage in front of my house when I got there.

"Hello, Fred," I said, startling him from his reverie.

He sat up straight, pushed his kipi back on his overgrown crop of wild blond hair, and grinned widely.

"Good afternoon, Herr Gatelatch," he said.

"What are you doing here?" I knew perfectly well what Fred Lundt was doing waiting in front of my house on the colonel's carriage.

"The colonel would like to talk with you," he replied happily.

"Climb on down from there, Fred, and come on inside the house. I've got to put all this stuff away."

He was quite happy to get out of the sun. "Been waiting long?"

"No." He watched me work the key in the lock. "Maybe I wait fifteen minutes. Frau Mullroy asked me inside but I told her I did not wish to miss you as the colonel would have my—how do you say—haut?"

"Hide."

"*Ja*. Hide."

Inside the house he swept off his hat and held it in both hands as he looked about curiously. Lundt was a tall, gangly boy—too tall really to be a good horse soldier but thin enough that he could sit an animal with all his gear and not exceed the weight limit.

He stood there looking around at my clutter of canvases, paints, and half-finished renderings while I deposited the easel and canvas in a corner and took the mesquite case into the back bedroom.

"There are some cookies on the table, Fred," I called out to him, shedding my warm jacket and flinging it onto the bed. "Help yourself."

The tin rattled. When I came out after changing my clothes and washing up, he was standing in the parlor with a cookie in each hand and what was left of a third in his mouth.

I grinned. It wasn't as if he'd been on maneuvers and had spent the last eight weeks living on salt pork, beans, and hardtack. Post food has never been long on variety or flavor even though it would keep a man alive…after a fashion. "Take some back with you," I offered.

"I want not to take too many," he said, crowding another cookie into his mouth.

"Don't worry, I always have plenty—too many," I added under my breath.

Lundt didn't need his arm twisted very far. He leaped upon the tin and crammed a handful of Tippi's oatmeal cookies into the pocket of his blouse and added three more to his left hand.

Tippi would approve.

I returned to the bedroom, tugged a comb through my hair, and told Lundt I was ready. As we headed for the door I noticed, in passing, the shiny bottom of the cookie tin showing through and the decidedly pregnant appearance of Lundt's pockets.

He had left me a few.

3

WE STOPPED at the door and Lundt rapped twice.

"Come in," said a voice from beyond.

Lundt turned the handle and pushed it open.

"Herr Gatelatch, sir," he said smartly.

Oliver Rundles looked across his cluttered desk where a field map was spread open and weighed down at the four corners by an assortment of objects picked off his desk: a stream-smoothed rock upon which were painted the words "I love you, Daddy. Jessica," a cigar box, his revolver, and a crystal glass holding water.

"Thank you, Private, you may go," he said.

Lundt saluted. Rundles liked to maintain a touch of formality while at post, but he was a smart enough commanding officer to allow certain things left behind when his men saddled up and rode out on a campaign. The door shut behind me and Rundles's stern mouth nudged up into a smile.

"Hello, Abe," he said, leaning back into his chair.

"Ollie," I said, pulling around another. I shook my head and said no thanks to the box of cigars he offered.

"Quitting?"

"Too early."

"It's never too early for a good cigar," he said, smoothing down the curled corner of the map and replacing the cigar box there.

Colonel Oliver Rundles was a husky man of forty-five. He had lived half his life atop a McClellan saddle and lost two fingers on his left hand to frostbite during the winter campaign of '76. Two years later a bitter Montana winter claimed several of his toes while pursuing renegade Sioux up along the Canadian border. But Ollie Rundles was U.S. Cavalry right down to his Fort Riley-issued socks, and he would gladly sacrifice the rest of his digits just for the pleasure of remaining on the open frontier. His eyes were blue and they had a habit of staring straight into yours when he spoke to you. His hair thinned back, exposing a shiny pate, and the fringe around his ears was beginning to gray.

On the wall behind him hung a map of Montana, Wyoming, and the Dakotas, and beside his desk stood a clay urn he had brought back from a tour of duty down in Arizona. A Sioux war lance protruded from the mouth of the urn. Scattered around it upon the wooden floor was a semicircle of fluffy gray ash.

Rundles peered at me across the clutter shoved aside to make room for the map, then said, "I sent a man out this morning to find you, Abe."

"I was working."

He grinned. "And I'll wager you didn't even touch a paintbrush."

"There are all different kinds of work, Ollie." I smiled cryptically.

"Yes, indeed, aren't there." He puffed on the cigar and flicked a long gray cylinder of ash toward the urn. "And from what I've been hearing, you best keep busy with your—er—work."

"Oh? What is it you've been hearing?"

"That Barrister McClain is in town, and that he is looking for you." He stabbed his cigar at me to emphasize the point.

The chair creaked under my weight as I leaned back in it. "Yes, I know. I saw him this morning."

"You saw him?" Concern leaped momentarily to Rundles's eyes. He grew uncomfortable in his chair. "I take it he didn't see you?" he said.

"No, he did not, and relax, Ollie. He doesn't know me by sight."

"No...I suppose not. Just the same, Abe, I think you ought to stay out of his way."

"I don't intend to go up to him and introduce myself, if that's what you mean."

"That isn't exactly what I mean." Rundles hesitated. "This might not be a bad time for you to leave town for a few days."

It was a terrible time for me to be leaving town for a few days. Barrister McClain was drinking hard and itching to gun someone down—me. If I was not around, whom would he find to vent his anger on? He was rabid mean when sober. Drunk, he made the devil look saintly.

"I don't know that that's such a good idea, Ollie," I said. "Riding out and leaving the town wide open for McClain doesn't make much sense, especially since it is me he's looking for."

Rundles looked disappointed. "I was afraid that was how you would see it." He came forward in his chair. "And that's exactly why you have to disappear for a while," he continued earnestly. He paused, then softened his position somewhat. "There is a sheriff in town, Abe. Barrister McClain is his problem."

I laughed. "Randy Linger is an untried, wet-behind-the-ears kid. He inherited a sack job from his father who never had to do any more than haul in Saturday night drunks and break up fistfights. If it wasn't that Randall is too crippled up with arthritis to hold a gun, he'd still be sitting behind the sheriff's desk. Randy has never had to deal with anything more than a few drunks. Sure, he can handle that sort of trouble just fine, but Barrister McClain is a whole different game. He'll chew Randy up and spit him out in little pieces if he tries to stand in his way."

"If that's true, Abe, do you think you could go up against the man?"

I didn't reply. Rundles knew the answer without me having to tell him.

I said, "If McClain wants me bad enough, he'll tear this town apart, and there is nothing any one man can do to stop him. You remember what his brother did in Billings?"

Rundles grunted.

"And Ryan McClain was a mere amateur when it came to such things. Barrister is the family top gun. I can't leave, not now, Ollie." Rundles knew it was true but I got the impression he was straddling the proverbial rock and hard place. He leaned back heavily into his chair and flicked another cylinder of ash toward the clay urn. There was regret in his eyes, and in his voice too when he spoke. "I'm afraid the decision is out of your hands, Captain," he said, using my rank to remind me that I was, after all, still in the cavalry…although unofficially. My peculiar position tended to isolate me from the formalities of saluting senior officers, wearing uniforms, and living rent-free on the post, but Colonel Oliver Rundles was still my commanding officer, and when he insisted, like any other soldier, I had to obey him.

"McClain doesn't even know what I look like," I said, trying to reason with him. "I'll stay low and keep an eye out for him. Chances are nothing at all will come of it."

"I understand your concern, Abe," Rundles said, "but what if McClain does start trouble and Randy isn't able to stop it?"

"Then I'd have to step in and handle it for him," I said, glancing away from his stabbing blue eyes.

He went on pressing his advantage. "And that is precisely why you have to get clear of town for a few days. The United States Cavalry has invested too much money and time in you, Abe. We've moved you into a convincing cover so that you can do things that the collective bumbling government bureaucrats tripping over their own red tape could never get done. One slip-up here where you live, where people know you as Abernathy Gatelatch, and all that would be lost."

"Not to mention the embarrassment the army would face trying to explain why they are keeping a noted gunfighter on the payroll," I observed. Every word he spoke was true. That didn't make leaving any easier.

He cleared his throat. "Yes, there is that too. If it will make you feel better," he hurried on, "I'll send in a couple troops to sort of keep an eye on things. Nothing official, mind you. Policing the town is beyond my jurisdiction, but a few armed soldiers won't draw attention and they'll be there in the event they are required."

"And what am I supposed to do? Just ride around and enjoy the countryside for the next two or three days?"

"I said nothing about giving you a vacation, Abe. I only said I wanted you out of town, and as it happens, I've got a job for you to do." He grinned and picked up a sealed brown envelope from his desk while sliding a finger across the map in front of him.

"How convenient," I said, leaning forward to see the name of the place his finger had settled upon.

4

"OH, MR. GATELATCH," Tippi hooted.

I stopped with my hand upon the doorknob.

Lundt was pulling away in the colonel's carriage. He turned at the sound of Tippi's voice, grinned sympathetically at me, then snapped the reins and directed his grin up the road.

Peering around the hydrangea bush by my front porch, I spied Tippi's happy, powdered face looking back at me from her front door.

"Evening, Tippi," I said, trying not to encourage her.

"You wait right there, Mr. Gatelatch," she said, ducking back inside her house. I drew in a breath and removed my hand from the doorknob. She reappeared a moment later with a basket covered by a red-and-white checked cloth.

I crossed the little yard and met her by the fence.

"I fried up some chicken this afternoon," she said, her pale eyes sparkling, "and I made some extra—just for you. I know how you bachelor boys are around the kitchen."

I wasn't a boy anymore, and I happened to be a fair hand around the kitchen when I put my mind to it, which wasn't very often, but the chicken smelled delicious and I was starved, so I didn't point this out to Tippi.

"Why, thank you very much." I lifted back a corner of the cloth and treated myself to a helping of the mouth-watering aroma. It was well after five o'clock and I'd missed lunch completely. Tippi was a wonderful cook; her fried chicken was superb, and I could always expect a basket of something special at least once a week—one of the advantages of being unmarried and living next door.

"What were you doing at the post?" she inquired casually, as if only politely interested, but I knew Tippi better than that. She'd been a sergeant's wife too many years; parade ground dust had gotten into her blood. Any news was big news to her; she relished it as some bachelors might relish a basket of her fried chicken. Tippi had loved living on the frontier almost as much as the Sergeant had. She took to it like a burrowing owl to a prairie dog hole and missed not being in the mainstream of army life.

"The colonel suggested a couple of paintings he'd like to have made to send back East to the War Department," I said, fighting back the first urges to salivate as the odor of warm fried chicken came up through the cloth.

"That's nice," she said, not overly thrilled at the news. She'd rather have heard what the colonel's wife was wearing, or the color of her new hat—or even if she had a new hat, but since I had not seen Irene Rundles, I couldn't help in that department. Tippi smiled, the creases deepening around her eyes.

I didn't particularly feel like smiling, thinking back over what the colonel had really called me in for, but I found one someplace and fixed it on my face. "I'll be leaving early in the morning to make some preliminary sketches."

"Will you be away long?" She tilted her head and hitched up an eyebrow.

"A few days, I should think."

"Then you will be back for the dance at the armory?" she said.

I'd nearly forgotten that. "Perhaps."

"Have you talked with Mary since this morning?" she asked offhandedly, distracted by a nonexistent spot on her blue dress, which she worked at for a moment with her fingernail.

"I haven't had time," I said, and wondered what excuse I might employ to extricate myself this time. I'd already lost the morning light. Perhaps an artist requires evening light as well? I was about to suggest it when she said:

"Well, you are in luck, Mr. Gatelatch." She forgot the spot on her dress in her enthusiasm.

"I happened to see Mary this afternoon while out shopping, and do you know what?"

I was afraid to ask. Fortunately, I didn't have to. It nearly bubbled out of her. "Mary said she'd be delighted to go to the dance with you Saturday night!"

"What! You asked her...for me?"

"Why—yes. I do hope that was all right. It is what you wanted, isn't it? After speaking with you this morning, I thought it would be all right just to mention it to her. We wouldn't want Mary to accept someone else's invitation before you had a chance to ask. I know how busy you always are, Mr. Gatelatch...It was all right, wasn't it?" She looked wounded.

My mind leaped ahead. Mary Landers was a charming girl—pretty, quiet, and helpful—but when it comes to asking young ladies to the armory dance, I sort of liked doing the asking myself. Tippi gave me her hurt-cow look.

"Er—yes—of course," I said, not wishing to hurt her feelings.

Tippi perked up. "That's wonderful! Mary is such a nice girl," we both said.

"Yes." She smiled serenely.

Tippi promised she would keep an eye on my house while I was away. I thanked her and carried the basket of chicken into the house, shut the door securely behind me, and leaned against it to think.

If I just didn't make it back by Saturday the problem would take care of itself, but then I'd have hurt feelings to contend with and besides, it seemed to me to be the coward's way out. No, if I got back before Saturday I'd have to escort Mary Landers to the dance…and what was so wrong with that? I asked myself, and couldn't come up with an answer. I gave the thought another moment to sift down through the gray matter then put it aside.

I set the basket atop the greatly depleted tin of cookies and slipped out of my jacket. The envelope Rundles had given me protruded from the inside pocket. I turned it toward the light coming through the windows.

It was addressed to Colonel William T. Hauser. I'd met Hauser briefly a few years back when I'd done a job for him that required crossing the Canadian border and bringing back an entrepreneur who had stolen a wagonload of munitions, mostly Springfield carbines and the .45-55 cartridges that went with them. The munitions had been en route to Fort Keogh, and Colonel Hauser had been its commanding officer. They ended up in the hands of Indians along the Canadian border. The entrepreneur, a disgruntled sutler named Renny Morgan, decided Canada wasn't such a bad place to stay. The cavalry couldn't touch him and Hauser wanted him, badly. I ended up bringing Morgan back, no questions asked.

Now Hauser was in a place I'd never heard of. Fort Avery was no more than a summer bivouac up along the Bitterroot Range. It would be abandoned come the winter snows.

I tapped the envelope upon my palm and wondered what was so important that it could not have been sent through regular military courier. Rundles had made a case for not wanting it to go with a uniformed patrol through Indian lands, but most of the nations were at peace now—a tenuous peace, certainly, but quiet nonetheless. Still, there were those occasional roving bands of renegades that Rundles felt would be attracted to a small column of men in blue. Well, perhaps he had a point.

"One man dressed in civilian clothing will be less conspicuous," he had said, glancing purposefully at the brown envelope just before handing it to me. "And, Abe," he went on with an intenseness in his eyes I had seldom seen before, "that message must get through to Colonel Hauser."

Well, if it was so important, I'd see that it got through to Hauser, but that didn't mean I had to like leaving now—now with Barrister McClain looking for me.

I tossed the jacket aside and dropped the brown envelope atop it, putting tomorrow's journey out of mind as I turned hungrily toward the basket. A delicious odor rushed out at me when I folded back the cloth. It teased my nose all the way to the kitchen table where I made short work of Tippi's fried chicken.

Able Gate

5

I TUCKED a scribbled thank-you note into the checkered cloth and left the empty basket on Tippi's front step. It was curiosity and a streak of plain stubbornness that didn't like being haltered by Rundles's advanced rank that pulled me toward town later that evening to see how it had weathered a day with Barrister McClain. I was pretty certain I knew where I would find him.

Mort Weaver was heading the same direction, and I fell in pace with him.

"Evening, Mort," I said.

He looked about, startled at finding me at his side; his mind had clearly been occupied elsewhere.

"Oh, Abernathy." He regained his composure and smiled. "I didn't hear you come."

"Lucky for you I'm a peaceable sort of fellow. How's it going?"

His smile changed directions. "I suppose you've heard what has been going on in town?"

"No, I've been out at the post most of the afternoon."

"You mean you don't know that Barrister McClain arrived this morning and he doesn't intend to leave until he finds that gunfighter, Able Gate?"

"Able Gate?" I said, awed. "Is he in town too?"

"I don't know, but McClain sure seems to think so."

"What is McClain doing about it?"

"Nothing much yet, except making threatening noises about what he's gonna do if Gate doesn't show his 'Chinaman yeller face' pretty soon."

"He said that?"

"Uh-huh. He's been holed up in the saloon all day, drinking like he got a sacred commission to dry up the town," Weaver said. "I told Berniece that she and the kids are not to come into town until that man leaves. So now guess what I'm doing?" Mort flourished a slip of paper and waved it in my face. "Berniece's shopping list. She said if she can't come in to do it then I was going to have to do it for her." He pouted and shoved the list back into his pants pocket.

I couldn't tell if Mort was more upset over doing Berniece's shopping or having McClain bivouacked in the saloon.

Mort yanked a watch from his vest pocket and snapped the lid open. "I've only fifteen minutes before Toby's Mercantile closes."

We quickened our pace.

"Has McClain caused any trouble?" I asked as he shoved the watch back into the pocket.

"Man, you have been out of town, haven't you?"

I shrugged my shoulders. "You know how it is when you live on a government retainer. When Ollie Rundles wants a new painting made to show off his spic-and-span command way out on the frontier to the people back East in the War Department who hold the purse strings, I have to jump and say 'yes sir,' just like the old days, heh?" I grinned to let him know I really didn't mind the work.

"I know how that is," Mort said. "I'm glad I'm out of it. Don't want to go back to that life no more neither." He shook his head. "Now whenever I shoe a horse the money goes into my pocket, and if I shoe a hundred horses I get paid for a hundred horses. In the cavalry it didn't matter how many nails I pounded or how many shoes I fitted. The pay was always the same, and they expected me to fight Injuns and live on hardtack to boot!"

"So, what's happening with McClain?"

"Oh, nothing much," Weaver went on. "Only he just threw two men into the middle of Main Street this morning and later in the afternoon he busted up another feller's arm— Sam Baxter—you know Sam, don't you?"

"Uh-huh."

"McClain busted his arm in two places and plunged him headfirst into the trough out front of the Custer. I've heard that that man was sober-mean, but when he gets drunk—" Mort shook his head.

I said, "What did Randy do about it?"

"Randy?" Weaver snorted. "That Linger kid got a piss-yellow streak up his back this wide. He suddenly discovered he had important business to tend to down at Crowley. He saddled up lightning quick this mornin' about ten o'clock...right after he realized that maybe he might have to do something to stop McClain from bustin' up this town. I'll say this, that boy ain't the sheriff old Randall was."

"He's still young," I said, "and his father never had to face a man like McClain. It's hard to say how he would have handled it."

"He wouldn't have rode out when we needed him," Mort said. "That boy shouldn't be our sheriff if he can't handle the job!"

I couldn't argue that, but until a man faces death, looks it in the eye with nothing separating him from it but the speed and accuracy of his gun, it's hard to say what he would do.

Randall Linger had faced death a time or two, but never death quite so sure as the variety Barrister McClain dealt out.

We came to Toby's Mercantile. Not having any place important to be at, and curious to hear more of the day's happenings, I accompanied Mort Weaver inside.

Spicy odors and the sharp bite of vinegar from open pickle barrels filled the air. Toby grinned at us from behind the counter, his white apron smudged and stained from the day's chores.

"Running late this evening, aren't we, gentlemen?"

"Taking care of some chores for Berniece," Mort said, wheeling toward the counter. I let him tend to his shopping and strolled over to examine some stiff, canvas work clothes. Footsteps stopped behind me.

"Mary?" I said, coming about. She was holding a bolt of yellow material in her arms and a bright smile was upon her face. I was a bit startled to find her standing there, and strangely pleased too. "Where did you come from?"

"I was over there when I saw you and Mr. Weaver come in."

I glanced to the window by the corner where colorful bolts of material were stacked on a shelf.

"Planning to do some sewing?"

"I'm always sewing something," she said, smiling. "Today I feel like sewing something special."

I was having an unusually difficult time regaining my composure, and I was uncertain why that should be. She stood there a moment looking pretty and expectant and I pretended not to notice either.

"Well," she said, the Fourth of July sparkles in her eyes fading after a few moments of uncomfortable silence, "I ought to finish my shopping before the store closes…"

I smiled foolishly and watched her turn away. If only the circumstances of my life were different, I thought, wishing Tippi would mind her own business and leave me alone. It occurred to me, too, that Rundles had picked a hell of a time to send me out on a mission—mission! I was being used as nothing more than a messenger boy, doing a job any raw recruit could handle!

"Mary," I said, dismay at the sound of my voice.

She turned and looked at me curiously.

I advanced a step, caught my hat in my fingers, and became aware of a lump left over from schoolboy days building unexpectedly and unwanted in my throat.

"Yes?"

"Are you planning to attend the armory dance?" I asked, knowing full well that she was. My sudden timidity annoyed me.

She glanced briefly at the bolt of material in her arms. "I was going to make a new dress for the dance—something special," she said with a certain tenseness that told me she, too, was suffering from the same flutter of butterflies.

We both knew what was to come next, and I suspect in our own ways we both wished Tippi still had a child of her own to mother instead of adopting the stray, unwed offspring of other folks.

I said, "Colonel Rundles has just told me he wants some sketches made for a couple paintings and I'm going to be leaving in the morning, but if I should get back by Saturday night I'd be pleased to escort you to the dance."

The story about going out to make sketches was a lie that over the years I had grown comfortable telling, but just now it left a foul taste in my mouth.

"I'd like that very much," she said, the Fourth of July returning to her eyes. "But do you really think you will be back by then?" I could see her dilemma. Accepting my invitation automatically cut off further offers. If I should be detained she'd have to go by herself or not at all. Either embarrassment or disappointment.

"I'll make a point of it," I said. That promise would mean a lot of hard riding. Suddenly it was not important. Strangely, the smile that presented itself to me was important.

Able Gate

6

I WALKED OUT of Toby's Mercantile like a boy of fifteen instead of a man of thirty-five, and I'd suddenly acquired a strange tolerance toward Tippi's matchmaking too.

On the boardwalk out front of Toby's, Mort peeled back toward the outskirts of town with his arms full of groceries and a severe tilt to his mouth when I told him I was going up to the Custer to see what's been going on.

"You best stay away from that place tonight, Abernathy," he advised. "I've a feeling there could be trouble, especially now that there ain't no sheriff in town."

"I'll be careful," I said, and watched him wrestle the packages down the street. I moved off casually in the direction of the saloon, stepped down into the long shadows that angled across the street, and paused by the batwings.

The piano in the corner was silent. The usual buzz of the busy saloon came instead as a whisper through the doors. I peered over them into the smoky interior. Barrister McClain was bent over the bar, an elbow propping up a whiskey glass. He tipped back his head, tossed the whiskey down, and swayed around on his heels. Then he spun around with catlike swiftness and flung the glass at the Franklin stove against the wall.

Clyde winced as it shattered but he said nothing.

A considerable pile of glass had already accumulated around that stove.

"More!" McClain rumbled.

Clyde Woolman levered himself out of the corner of the bar where he had been standing looking very unhappy and approached Barrister, wiping sweaty hands upon his apron. He removed a fresh glass from in front of the mirror and reached under the bar for a bottle.

McClain snatched the bottle from him, yanked the cork out with his teeth, and spat it at the mirror. Whiskey splashed across the bar as he attempted to pour it into the glass.

McClain set the bottle down and glared at me when I pushed aside the doors and stepped in. His narrowed eyes followed me to the table where three men that I knew sat. The saloon was practically empty; the only sound at the moment was the slow ticking of a clock. Making a brief head count, I judged it was twenty or thirty short of the usual number for a Monday evening. Another reason for the unhappy expression on Clyde's face.

"Hullo, Abernathy," Clarence Wimble said in a subdued voice, void of its usual enthusiasm.

"Evening, Clarence…Walt, Andrew." I nodded around the table, pulled back a chair.

"What brings you out and about tonight?" Andrew Sorbel asked.

"Same as you, I suppose."

He grinned and said, "You know what they say about curiosity. I guess there are more than a few of us here for that reason."

"I came to see what a notorious killer looks like," Walt Teral said, leaning across the table, and I could see he had already had too much to drink. "He don't look so tough, do he?" he said, but he didn't say it very loudly.

"Don't get any foolish ideas thinking that liquor has slowed him up," Clarence said. "That man could beat your hand a dozen times over, even twice as drunk as he is now."

That didn't sit well with Walt, who fancied himself a hand with a gun. Like McClain, Walt was working up a good hangover himself.

"Don't start riding me, old man," he said in hushed anger. Walt was the only man in the saloon fool enough to be wearing a gun. That made me a tad nervous, as Walt did not have a reputation for being a prudent lad. He was a young fellow, not yet twenty-five, and he had a habit of going off halfcocked when angered.

"I didn't mean anything by it," Clarence said. "The point is, that fellow at the bar has so much of the devil in him that you could shoot him three times and he'd never feel it—it wouldn't stop him from plugging you before he died."

"That's right," Andrew added. "You can't kill men like that without getting hurt in the bargain. He isn't worth it."

"I didn't mean for it to sound like it did," Clarence said. "Andrew is right, he ain't worth getting killed over."

Walt frowned. "It's all right," he said, fingering an empty glass in front of him. "I never said I wanted to go against him, only that he didn't look so tough."

Walt must have had more to drink than I had guessed because Barrister McClain looked plenty tough to me. I said, "I heard he busted up Sam Baxter pretty badly."

"Uh-huh," Andrew said. "Sam had him a few drinks and decided someone ought to tell McClain the way folks feel about him being in town. You know how Sam gets when he'd had a few too many drinks."

"Sam was lucky," I said.

They mumbled their agreements with me. Clyde Woolman came over looking like a wet cat.

Clarence said, "What's the matter, Clyde, business take a plunge?"

"I sure wish that feller would pack up and leave," Clyde said under his breath—and then louder, "Can I get you boys anything?"

I said, "No, thanks." This was the sort of night that required a clear head.

Obviously Walt didn't agree. "I'll have another, Clyde," he said.

I spied a worried flash in Clarence's eyes but he did not say anything. Both he and Andrew waved their hands over their empty glasses and shook their heads. Clyde went back to the bar, unhappy about life, liberty, and the pursuit of happiness—at least the way McClain was pursuing his happiness.

Walt said, "I don't know why everyone is pretending this is a funeral. I think it's kinda excitin'."

"You would," Andrew said softly. Walt missed it.

Clarence made an effort to switch the subject onto a different track. "So, what's new in the world of art, Abernathy?" he said, looking at me.

I shrugged, smiled, and put my back to Barrister McClain as if he were of no particular concern of mine. "It's looking pretty good. Colonel Rundles just commissioned two more paintings for the War Department. I'm going to be leaving in the morning to make some preliminary sketches."

"Well, good for you, Abernathy." Clarence tried to sound enthusiastic, but his world revolved around cows, not art.

Walt looked at me and said, "I reckon you won't be around for the dance, then, will you, Abernathy?"

There was a challenge in his words, but my plans weren't any of his business. I said, "I haven't thought that far ahead."

"Well, I have," he went on, grinning drunkenly. "I've been thinking about it a whole lot, and I decided I'm a going to offer my services to that cute little Mary Landers and then maybe later, after the dance, persuade her to go for a walk behind the livery where Chester piles the new hay." He chuckled and his eyebrows arched wickedly.

I didn't like the smile that widened his smooth face.

Andrew was laughing softly. "Boy, you'll be lucky if Mary agrees to one dance with the likes of you."

"I'll get a lot more than one dance off of Mary"—he smirked confidently—"and that's a promise, Andrew, old man."

"Shut up," I said in a low, even voice that startled them all...including me. I'd stepped momentarily out of character and covered it over with a grin, but it came off more like a snarl, which only incensed Walt further.

Walt said, "You listen to me, Mr. Art Man, I don't like being told to shut up, especially by a funny little man who paints pictures for a living!"

Walt Teral was taller than I, and a bit broader in the shoulders too, but in my book that only meant there was too much of him for him to make it in the cavalry. It was no indication of prowess in any way. I thought of Colonel Rundles, who was a good two inches shorter than I. I've seen Rundles fight like a compact mama bear protecting cubs and I didn't figure Walt's height or his weight would swing much of an advantage over an angry Ollie Rundles, or even over a half-angry "funny little man who paints pictures for a living."

But Walt was drunk and this wasn't the time or the place to let his temper turn to blows—not with Barrister McClain suddenly taking an interest in our little squabble.

McClain was watching us over his right shoulder. After giving it some thought, he straightened himself up, wrapped his fingers around the whiskey glass, and threaded a wavering line in our direction.

He hovered over us like a buzzard circling carrion. "I'm looking for a no-good son of a bitch named Able Gate." His dark eyes had fixed themselves somewhere in the middle of our table. "Any of you know where he can be found?" He stabbed back a foot to arrest motion in that direction, straightened himself up, and considered each one of us intently. Even so, I had a feeling he'd not remember any one of us come morning when, most likely, the only thing he'd be looking for was a dark hole to curl up in and die.

Standing there, Barrister McClain was even bigger than he had appeared this morning atop his gray mare—definitely not cavalry material. He wore a long, black frock coat that smelled of sweat and whiskey and atop his head sat a black, flat-brimmed hat growing a white, salt rime around the base of its crown. His sun-ravaged face had had its features carved into it with the blunted point of a pickax: facial topography that the graying stubble of a beard followed like lichen growing into the irregularities of a shattered rock. He would have filled a doorway passing through, and I suspected he'd be hard as a grizzly bear to stop.

"You tell me where I can find him," he growled, his words slurred. "The son of a bitch gunned down my brother, Ryan. I mean to take his head back with me on a stick or pull this town down looking for him."

Andrew shook his head and said, "I've heard of this man, Able Gate, but he doesn't live here."

McClain's hand came down and gathered up a fistful of shirt. He yanked Andrew out of his chair. "I'll hang your head on that stick, right beneath Gate's, if you're talking crossways with me, mister. Yours and anyone else's who gets in my way!"

Andrew crashed back into his chair and McClain turned on us. "If any one of you knows where Gate is, you best tell me now." He stood there, his red eyes boring holes into us, then turned on his heels and stomped back to the bar, pausing midway to fling the empty glass at Ben Franklin.

"Another!" he snarled.

Clyde unhappily left his corner.

Andrew straightened up in the chair indignantly. "What makes him so damned certain this Able Gate fellow is here, in our town?"

"Well, how do we know he ain't?" Walt said. "Who of us even knows what Able Gate looks like?"

We all immediately looked at Walt. I had the uneasy feeling that his comment had been a poison dart secretly hurled at me, perhaps because at the moment Walt's angry eyes had locked on to mine.

"Walt has got a point," Clarence said.

I shook my head. "If someone of Able Gate's reputation lived here among us, don't you think we'd all know about it?"

"I don't know," Andrew said, still vibrating from his encounter with Barrister McClain. "If he did live here I'd say he'd be extra careful not to draw attention to himself. After all, wouldn't he want a safe place to come back to, a place where he could walk the streets and enjoy a drink with friends…don't you think?"

I squirmed in my chair.

"That's right," Walt said, eyeing me again. He glanced away when I looked straight at him.

Clyde came over and placed a fresh whiskey in front of Walt.

"You okay, Andrew?" Clyde said.

"Yes, I'm…I'm fine."

"I wish I knew how long he intends to stand there drinking my whiskey and smashing my glasses. What will he do when I run out of one or the other?"

I said, "Looks like you've got an all-nighter on your hands, Clyde."

"Maybe Randy will get back soon." Clyde wiped the sweat from his palms on the apron.

Walt laughed into his whiskey.

Clyde shook his head and wandered dolefully back to the bar. Walt was hiding a grin in his glass.

I said, "Don't you think you've had enough of that stuff tonight?"

He set the glass down with a bang.

McClain looked over his shoulder.

"I don't think it's none of your business, Gatelatch," he said sharply.

At the bar McClain had straightened around and was looking at me.

"Keep your fool voice down," Andrew cautioned, trying not to be too obvious as he glanced at the bar.

"Well, you just tell Mr. Art Man there to start minding his own business!" Walt tossed down the rest of his drink and stood. He leaned forward, planting his fists on the table and putting his face close to mine.

"I'm gonna roll Mary Landers this Saturday night, Mr. Art Man, and I don't give a damn what you think about it." He grinned suddenly and stood. "You just remember that come Saturday when you're out painting your pretty pictures...Mr. Art Man."

Walt walked unsteadily for the door and disappeared into the night.

"He's just drunk," Clarence said at my elbow.

"That's right," Andrew added. "He's just making big noises."

I watched him disappear into the darkness outside. When I turned back McClain's head was cocked in my direction.

7

OLLIE RUNDLES was true to his word.

I spied them when I left the Custer Saloon a few minutes behind Walt Teral, standing nonchalantly up the road by a dark hitching rail, talking, apparently, about the bright sprinkle of stars overhead and not at all concerned over who went into or came out of the saloon. I paused on the boardwalk outside and inhaled air free of cigar smoke and stale whiskey, and glanced their way. Although they appeared to be loitering, they were there for a reason.

With the post only a mile or so out of town, there were always troopers in town, but these three were different. They were armed—a subtle distinction easily overlooked by anyone who didn't know what was going on.

I grinned into the darkness. Rundles was keeping his eye on things while Randy was away. I glanced back at the man leaning against the bar and felt just a little bit better about leaving in the morning.

The clear, cool night was a pleasant reprieve from the hot summer day that had preceded it, and I headed home trying not to think about Barrister McClain or Walter Teral or the long ride come morning. I did, however, allow Mary Landers room in my thoughts, and that quite naturally pulled Walt into them also. Whether his designs on Mary were the idle talk of a drunken brain, or there was some deep-seated plan to harm her, I couldn't be sure, but thinking about it twisted a knot of concern in my stomach. I was allowing the kid to get to me. I'd already promised Mary I'd be back by Saturday, so I didn't see any point of dwelling on it. I shoved them both out of mind as I turned the corner.

I stopped quite suddenly then, not knowing why. I listened to the sounds of my breathing, the sounds of my feet upon the ground, and heard nothing else, yet the hairs at the back of my neck had begun to bristle. I peered into the shadows that grew up alongside dark buildings and warily started again toward home, wondering what it was that had set off the alarms inside my head.

I took another couple of steps when the voice called out from the darkness.

"Mr. Art Man," it slurred.

I stopped and turned slowly in the direction of the voice. A dark shape separated itself from the shadows. I didn't have to see his face.

"Pleasant evening, isn't it, Walt," I said amiably, noting that his right hand was hovering near the butt of his revolver.

He advanced another step and halted in the open where the moon's gray light reached down to wash out his features.

"You want to tell me again that I've had too much to drink, Mr. Art Man, now that you ain't got no friends around to cover for you?"

I didn't recall anyone covering for me back in the saloon, but I figured in Walt's present condition that would be a moot point.

"No, I don't want to tell you that, Walt. We really ought to talk about this some other time, when you're sober."

"No, we're gonna talk now."

"You're drunk," I said, noticing the hammer thong dangling from his holster. I was unarmed and it wasn't a good time to provoke him.

He came forward again and stopped three feet in front of me, his drunkenness heavy on his breath. Walt was young and strong and whiskey-bold; mix them together and you get an explosive situation.

"Good night, Walt." I turned my back to him and every fiber in my body went taut. I didn't expect just to walk away like that, but it was worth a try. Walt Teral was a proud and angry man but he wasn't a killer, and I figured he'd use his fists before going for the gun.

His hand came down on my shoulder like a smithy's vise and turned me around. I came about already calculating where his first blow might land and made a point of not being there to receive it.

Bunched knuckles sliced the empty air where a moment before my face had been and, reluctantly, I came back with a short jab that buckled him forward.

The wind went out of him and in that moment there opened before me any number of avenues to finish off the kid properly. But I had no great dislike for Walt. He was drunk and bothersome now, but he'd always been a likable kid, if not a little brash at times. A couple more years under his belt was all he needed to knock down the rough edges.

I left him buckled and hugging his gut, puffing like a locomotive.

"We'll talk about this some other time," I said, and turned back toward home. Behind me Walt sucked in a sharp breath of air.

"Gatelatch!" he hissed. The sound of his gun leaving its holster and the distinctive four clicks of a Colt's hammer being drawn back to full cock followed.

I heaved myself headlong into the street as the thunderous roar of the .45 tore a hole in the silence of the night and three feet of orange flame leaped out at me.

He lost me in the shadows and stood there with the revolver cocked for a second try, swaying unsteadily. I lay stone still in the darkness beneath a hedge watching his face change from anger to uncertainty and then concern.

"Gatelatch?"

I gathered up a small pebble and tossed it out into the street. He swung toward the sound raising the gun, but Walt wasn't a killer. He didn't have the proper instincts for it. He was just angry at the moment, and frightened. His first shot had stunned him, had taken most of the fight from him. He stood there with the gun outstretched but not pulling the trigger.

He was confused, too, and I took that moment to spring, knocking the gun from his hand in one move while bringing my fist up.

His teeth crashed together and he stumbled backward, sprawling into the street. I scooped up his pistol and ejected the cartridges into my palm.

Walt groaned and sat up holding his jaw with both hands. When he looked at me there was a dark trickle down his chin and a wide confusion in his eyes. After all, what did a "funny little man who paints pictures for a living" know about self-defense?

I had the uneasy feeling that Rundles had been right. Maybe it was time for me to distance myself from this place for a while. At least until McClain had cleared out and now until Walt cooled down.

But the notion of leaving, with Barrister McClain in town, struck me a little like allowing a rattlesnake in the nursery while the baby played on the floor.

Walt rubbed his chin, sleeved away the blood, and just sat there looking up. The curtained windows of the houses around us had remained dark, and I didn't feel like standing in the middle of the street waiting for someone to get curious about a gunshot in front of their home.

"How in blazes...!" Walt began, then winced and clutched his jaw again. He dabbed at the blood.

"We can talk about it later, when you feel more like talking," I said, tossing him the pistol. "Now get on home, Walt, and put yourself to bed."

He plucked the gun up from the dirt and fumbled it back into his holster. He stood uncertainly, looked at me with a mixture of surprise and hate, then moved off up the street.

He turned the corner and I frowned. He was going the wrong way, heading back into town for more whiskey...and maybe a run-in with McClain if he wasn't careful.

Well, Walt was a big boy now. You can help a person only so far and then you have to let them go it on their own. Clarence had taken over the role of father and advisor after Walt's parents had died, and I had tried to be his friend, but neither of us had the right to tell him how to live his life. That was something he'd have to learn for himself. I only hoped he didn't get himself killed before the lessons were over.

Dropping the cartridges from his revolver in my pocket and snatching my hat from off the ground along the way, I turned homeward again.

Able Gate

8

PRIVATE LUNDT pulled up early the following morning in Colonel Rundles's carriage. I let the curtain drop back in place, gathered up my gear, and dumped the remaining oatmeal cookies from the tin into a brown paper bag. After enough miles of dust and sun and rain, even oatmeal cookies can start to look good.

"Gut morning, Herr Gatelatch," Lundt said as I hauled my gear to the carriage.

"Morning, Fred." I stowed the case behind the seat and climbed aboard. To the east the first light of morning was spreading in a rosy hue above the low hills.

"More special work for the colonel?"

"That's right."

I settled in the seat and noticed that Lundt was trying hard to guard his smile. He snapped the reins and the carriage lurched forward. My position with the cavalry was not supposed to be general knowledge among the troops, but it's difficult to disguise my regular comings and goings completely, and suspicions grew like bindweed through a garden. They were shrewd enough, however, not to let the rumors spread beyond the mess hall and barracks.

I told my usual story about the colonel wanting another couple of paintings made to send back to Washington.

Lundt was polite enough to pretend he believed me.

When we pulled into the parade grounds, he toed the brake and hauled back on the reins in front of the commandant's office.

"He is waiting for you."

"Thanks, Fred."

I lifted the heavy mesquite case out of the carriage and carried it up to the door and knocked.

"Come in, it's open," Rundles said.

Inside, I shut the door and set the case on the floor.

"Coffee?" he asked, lifting a silver cup from a silver service set. Rank has its privileges.

"Sure."

"You all ready?"

"No."

He grinned and handed me the silver cup. "The town will still be here when you get back, Abe."

"But, we hope, not McClain?" I said.

"We hope. Have you eaten?"

"No."

"I'll have something sent up from the mess hall."

Rundles stepped outside and I moved my gear into the back room where I changed into clothes more suitable for travel. I packed away the window-glass spectacles and tugged a weathered hat on my head of proper proportions to keep the harsh Montana sun off my face and neck. I shed the jacket and slipped into a vest, finally strapping the gun around my waist.

When I returned, Rundles was seated behind his desk sipping coffee. At a knock at his door, he motioned me back into the back room. When I stepped out again a tray of bacon and eggs and toast waited on a large green metal tray.

"Eat up," Rundles said. "It may be the last decent meal you have for a few days."

I grinned at him. "Since when has the cavalry started serving decent meals, Ollie?"

He chuckled.

The horse that waited behind his office was wearing my personal saddle and saddlebags. Ollie kept them well stocked with the necessities a traveling man would need, as only a well-trained cavalry man could, and I often wondered how he explained that to the men in the stables. The horse was a strong animal I'd used a time or two in the past. It lacked the usual U.S. Government brand, and I wondered how he explained that away too. But I've never asked. We all have our little secrets.

I slipped the Springfield into the saddle scabbard and swung a leg over. It felt good to be astride an animal again; the role I played out in town as Abernathy Gatelatch was quite unsatisfactory in many respects. Having to rent a buggy whenever I wanted to go anywhere was only one of them. There were other disadvantages...My mind took a leap from reality and for a moment I was thinking about Mary Landers and frowning.

"Take care, Abe."

Rundles's voice brought me back to the job at hand.

"I make a point of that," I said, and adjusted the revolver to a comfortable place on my hip.

He heaved open a narrow side gate behind the row of buildings. I turned the horse out the gate and nudged it into an easy lope. When I glanced back the gate was closed and Rundles gone.

I angled to the northwest and deliberately put McClain, Teral, and Mary out of mind, turning my attention instead to the hills ahead and the letter in my pocket that Oliver Rundles thought was too important to trust to the regular military courier service.

The sun rose above the hills like a bright sunflower in August and I rode away from the fort, across a land that only ten short years ago had been hostile Indian Territory. It had not been much more than a dozen years ago that Lieutenant Colonel Custer had made his fatal error, and that, I suppose, more than anything, had accelerated the movement of the Indian population off the land and onto the reservations. Who could have guessed that the Sioux's greatest victory would sound the final death knell of their freedom?

Custer had been the unifying factor, the excuse. But the real reason the Sioux had to go was the gold and silver. The problem was keeping the white man off Indian land and not Indians off white man's land. The cavalry's initial job was hauling bonanza-seeking miners out, not fighting Indians. It only degenerated into that later. In the end it even became fashionable in the eyes of the white eastern population to remove Indians instead of careless and thoughtless miners.

Behind me, the town and fort dropped from view and wide, rolling grasslands opened up ahead. It gave a man a sense of freedom. Astride a good horse, there were no boundaries a man could not cross, except those he set for himself.

The sun arched higher. Shadows shortened. I removed the vest under the heat of a noonday sun and squinted at the hazy, purple saw-tooth range that had begun to rear its head above the horizon.

Evening's coolness brought me into the broken shelf land of the foothills. The ride had been easy, uneventful, and I was weary from the late night before. Perhaps if I wasn't so certain Rundles had sent me out on a wild-goose chase just to get me out of town, I'd have taken the job more seriously. As it was, I felt I was just marking time.

If I had taken it seriously, I might have kept my brain alert instead off chasing daydreams and pondering the shifting hues across the landscape as the sun completed its crescent and dipped down toward the mountains that had been drawing nearer all day.

Perhaps then I would have been aware of the odor of smoke and correctly identified its meaning before I rode into their camp completely unaware.

As it was, my first indication that I was not alone was the double-barrel shotgun that appeared in front of my nose.

9

"GIT DOWN offa that horse, mister," he said after we both surmounted our initial surprise at running into each other out there where the chances of riding accidentally into another man's camp ranged from slight to none at all.

"Take it easy with that scattergun, friend."

"I ain't your friend, mister." His thin lips pulled back, revealing broken and missing teeth embedded in reddened gums. The action deepened the crow's feet at the corners of his eyes. He danced nervously on the balls of his feet as if his boots were infested with critters that crawled and bit, and indeed they might have been. His finger twitched about the trigger of the short gun that was pressed into his slight shoulder. He squinted along the top of its barrels as if, at this close range, it was necessary to take careful aim at me.

Behind him a circle of black rocks contained the remains of a fire. A charred coffeepot, tilted against the rocks, was banked about with the coals. Beyond it sagged two sun-rotting canvas tents, and around the tents lay the garbage of a well-established camp. Pack frames, boxes, and rusty tools lay scattered about. Alongside the nearer tent was a growing pile of refuse that, even at a distance, I could see was comprised largely of human excrement.

A movement in one of the tents caught my eye. When I looked the tent flap settled back in place.

Beyond the camp large blocks of land tilted and uplifted out of the earth. Into the side of these cliffs a hole had been excavated. The waste from that hole fanned away out front of the opening in a broad sweep of red and gray rock.

"I ain't gonna tell you again, mister, now git on offa that horse." He was beginning to sweat.

"All right," I said, "ease off of that trigger." I swung off the horse and kept the reins in hand as a way of assuring the nervous gent that I wasn't planning to reach for my own gun.

"Now the gun belt." He motioned at it with the shotgun.

I undid the buckle and lowered the belt to the ground at his feet. That seemed to ease his tension some, and the shotgun moved from his shoulder.

"Now step back a pace or two."

As I did so the tent flap parted and a flash of pink appeared, receding almost immediately into the darkness inside.

He plucked my gun belt from the dirt and waved his gun toward the camp.

"Over there."

I took the reins and he followed behind me at a healthy distance.

"What's your name, mister?" he asked.

"Abernathy. Abernathy Gatelatch."

"All right, Mr. Abernathy Gatelatch, you can stop right there."

I stopped.

"Now sit down."

It seemed the prudent course to follow with him holding all the hardware. I lowered myself to the ground where he indicated and discovered to my left a thick, wooden stake that had been driven into the hard earth. To it was nailed a chain that trailed away along the ground and into the tent with the closed flap.

He took my horse to a picket line and tied it off.

"Carl! Carl, come on out here!" he said over his shoulder at the hole in the cliff.

We waited, and then—

"Yeah, what is it you want, Weevil?"

A form separated itself from the deeper shadows of the mineshaft and stepped out into the low afternoon sunlight. He wore baggy overalls and a sweat-soaked red Union shirt. On his head was a battered brown hat, and his fist clutched the handle of a pickax.

"What is it you want now, Weevil?"

He cut off his words, shaded his eyes with the flat of his hand, and squinted at me. "Who you got there?"

"This feller jest rode into camp."

"Why didn't you shoot him?"

Weevil's thin shoulders shrugged and he looked embarrassed. "I don't know, Carl. I figured we best learn who he was and how he found us. If he knows where we was maybe someone else knows too."

Carl thought this over and agreed reluctantly. He swung the pickax lightly in his hand as he came over to peer down at me. I could see that he was thinking, but seemingly having some problems in that department. "What's your name?" he asked.

"It's Gatelatch, Carl. I already asked him."

"Well, now I'm a-askin' him. What's your name?"

"Gatelatch."

"See?"

"Shut up, Weevil." He thought a moment. "That's a strange name, ain't it? Gatelatch?"

"I had nothing to do with it," I said. "I sort of inherited it."

"Don't go sassing me, mister!" The pickax came up menacingly, then he reined back on his temper and let the ax come to rest on the ground again.

"Who told you where to find us? Huh? Was it Cary? Huh?"

"I don't know anyone named Cary."

"Then it was someone else. Who?"

I briefly considered telling him that I had just stumbled upon their precious camp and I would be pleased just to stumble on out again, but then I reconsidered deciding that such an admission of ignorance might prove swiftly fatal.

"Who told you?" His anger flared and the pickax came up again in sudden, uncontrollable rage. There was nothing more he'd like to do than smash my head with it.

Weevil came up alongside him. "Cary wouldn't tell," he said.

Carl's frantic eyes glanced at him. "I wouldn't put it past that kid, not when he's been drinking and trying to impress the women."

"Aw, Cary knows better than to talk. He wouldn't say nothing, even to impress the skirts."

"You say that 'cause Cary's your brother's boy, but I never did trust him none too much."

Weevil stuck his finger up his nose then wiped it on his shirt. "He's my kin, Carl, and I'm not certain I like you bad-mouthin' him like that."

Carl turned on him. "The truth to tell, Weevil, I'm not sure I trust you none too much neither."

Weevil said, "Well, wasn't it me what found this strike?"

"We both found it."

"No, Carl, you was up over the ridge adiggin' when I struck color down here."

"That ain't what I meant. I meant we both come out together."

"So why don't you trust me?"

"'Cause you talk too much."

"I talk too much? Who was it that went abraggin' to that Injun about the strike we made up in these hills? Huh, Carl? It weren't me and it weren't Gary neither," Weevil said.

A crack appeared in Carl's offensive. He glanced at me, embarrassed, then looked back at Weevil. His voice had lost some of its sand.

"Well, I made it right, didn't I?"

Weevil huffed. "Yeah, you made it right all right. You killed the Injun. But that ain't the point. The point is, when it comes to talkin' your mouth off, you done a hell of a fine job of it. It weren't Cary or me who did the blabberin'."

As they were carrying on, I heard a metallic rattle and watched the chain shift minutely across the ground. Something inside the tent brushed against one of the canvas sidles, and I began wondering what sort of animal they had in there. The thickness of the chain immediately ruled out anything as large as a bear, and it had to be something accommodating enough to allow a human in with it too, I decided, recalling the face that had peeked out at my arrival.

As the two of them argued the shotgun in Weevil's hand left me, and I calculated the distance to my horse and the Springfield it carried. Ruefully I determined it was too far.

They were still at each other when a freight wagon appeared on the ridge behind them and slowly rumbled down into their camp. It was pulled by two tired horses with dull brown coats stretched so tight they were seemingly the only things keeping all their ribs bundled together. "Here comes Cary now," Weevil said.

"It's about time. Next time I'll go in for the supplies, and I don't care how much he bitches about me cutting into his love life."

"Why should you?" Weevil said. "You got yours stashed right handy. A kid his age needs the attentions of a woman."

"Then let him bring him one out here," Carl said. He wheeled around and said to me, "I'll get back to you later, mister. Weevil, see that he gets tied up proper."

Carl strode over to meet the wagon while Weevil saw to it that I got tied up proper.

"Hullo, Carl," the young man said, grinning down from the wagon.

"What took you so damned long?"

The grin spread. "I had me some personal business to tend to."

Cary swung off the wagon and he and Carl hauled a heavy box out the back and set it on the ground near the fire pit.

"Where's the money?"

Cary patted the lump in his pocket. "Right here. Three hundred and twenty dollars. Not bad for a week's work."

"Three hundred and twenty? I figured more than that."

Cary shrugged. "Assayer says we hit a streak of lower-grade ore."

Suspicion deepened in Carl's face. "Let me see it."

Cary dug the pouch out of his pocket. The coins tumbled into Carl's palm; shiny yellow as they come from the mint. The sight of the gold diminished his doubts, and he tumbled them over in his hand grinning.

"They look real pretty, don't they, Cary, all them eagles shining like a new day's sun." He funneled them back into the pouch and hid them away in his own pocket.

"The man at the assay office says we ought to file a legal claim on our strike. He says we're foolish not to. He says if we don't have the legal papers on it, someone could file on it and take it away from us."

Carl shook his head. "Soon as we tell the location every claim-jumpin' buzzard in the territory will be trying to steal it from us. I got me a gun and that's better than any piece of paper. I'd like to see anyone try to take this here claim from us."

Cary grinned. "The man at the bank offered me fifty dollars if'n I'd tell him where our claim was."

"What you say?"

"I told him he could go visit the devil."

Carl eased back. Weevil joined them, tickling his eyeball through his nose. "Got him all trussed up," he said.

That was a fact. He'd bound my hands behind me and tied off the end of the rope to the stake. I counted it fortunate that the sun was on its way down. It gave me several hours of darkness to work on the problem of escape. Come morning this piece of open ground would become one hot hunk of real estate.

At Weevil's words Cary noticed me sitting there. "Where did he come from?"

"That's what I'd like to know," Carl said.

"He just rode into camp 'bout half an hour ago," Weevil said, continuing a tactile exploration of his nasal cavity.

"I've been trying to make him tell who told him about this place," Carl said.

Cary came near and looked down at me as if I were a strange animal that had crawled out from under a rock.

"What did he tell you?" he asked, hunkering down to study me from a different angle.

"He ain't said nothing yet," Carl said. "At first we kinda thought you had mouthed off."

"Me?" Cary laughed, and looked purposefully back at me. I grinned at him but he didn't seem to notice.

He fingered a pebble and tossed it at me, experimentally, as if prodding a rattlesnake in a wagon rut to see if it was dead or alive.

I dodged it and that brought a satisfied grin to his face. He found a bigger rock and tried harder. It stung into my shoulder. He enjoyed that and searched the ground again.

"Aw, leave him alone for now," Weevil said. "We can talk to him after dinner. I'm astarvin'. Where is that woman anyway?" He turned to the tent and said, "Kenshoo, git your butt out here and fix us somethin' to eat."

A woman appeared at the doorway of the first tent. Her face was sunburned and dirty and her long hair hung down her back in twisted, matted knots. Weariness showed in her movements as she cowered out of the tent like a dog that had seen the end of a stick one too many times. She was dressed in filthy buckskins that at one time had been adorned with bright beadwork. Now all that remained of it was a few red and blue beads and a lot of frayed thread. As she moved I noticed how the material of her dress stretched across her stomach.

She was with child, and well along.

And then I noticed something else too. An iron shackle was attached to a red and swollen ankle, and the chain moved across the ground as she limped toward the fire.

10

THE KNOTS HELD tight against my bunched wrists. The only result of my efforts was raw skin from the coarse hemp fibers. After a while I stopped trying. I didn't really expect to find much give in Weevil's handiwork. Carl had told him to tie me up proper, and he had done so. Just the same, it was worth a try.

Kenshoo stood back as Carl hauled an armful of wood over to the fire. She did not look at him. She did glance sideways at me, but she was keeping her curiosity well-guarded.

Carl dropped the wood by the fire pit and she immediately set to work building up the fire, stirring the embers into a display of sparks that crackled skyward from the circle of rocks. Having laid the wood in, she turned to the large box Cary and Carl had deposited earlier and began sorting through the groceries.

Cary came over to me and hunkered down again. I half expected him to pick up a rock, but instead he studied me silently.

"Who are you really?" he said finally in an easy voice. "Uncle Weevil says your name is Gatelatch." He gave me a grin to show me he didn't really believe that story.

"Would your uncle lie to you?"

"No, he wouldn't, but you'd lie to him."

Under all the dirt, Cary was a good-looking boy, still young enough to have all his teeth, but that wouldn't last long if he continued in the habits of his uncle…and he was definitely following in Weevil's footsteps.

The wind shifted and the stench rolled over me. Whatever the personal business was he had taken care of in town, bathing hadn't been part of it.

"It's the name my father gave to me," I said, "the only one I've ever had." I didn't think this was the time to tell him who I really was. I knew nothing about Cary—except he didn't bathe and enjoyed throwing stones—but if he ever had an urge to acquire a reputation secondhand, it wouldn't be any easier than now. He could shoot me here where I sat and then haul me into town on his wagon and explain to everyone how he had outgunned me.

"What is it you do, Gatelatch?" he asked after a moment's thought.

"I'm an artist."

"A what? Uncle Weevil, you hear that? This fellow says he's an artist."

"Don't listen to him, boy. He's a claim jumper and he's alying to you."

"You draw pictures?"

"Uh-huh."

"Can you draw me a picture?"

"Not with my hands tied."

"Yeah, I guess not. Well, maybe some other time." He stood and shuffled back to the fire with his hands thrust deep into his pockets.

I was thinking that Cary had picked a strange way to end the conversation when out of the corner of my eye I saw

Kenshoo watching me. She averted her eyes when I looked at her. How much of what was said had she understood? By her clothes I judged her to be Sioux, but something about her didn't ring true, something I couldn't put a finger on.

She moved to the food box, dragging the chain after her. Although she did not complain, a spasm at the corner of her mouth indicated that the raw skin under the iron anklet was causing more than mild discomfort.

I tried to make myself comfortable on the ground with little success and watched her prepare their dinner.

The food smelled delicious to a hungry man but I was offered no part of it. That was just as well, as I doubted I could have eaten any. I wasn't hungry enough yet. I'm sure the Indian woman did a fine job of preparing it, considering what she had to work with. It was what she had to work with that turned my stomach.

Perhaps water was scarce, or perhaps they just didn't care. Whatever the reason, their utensils had enough crusted-over food left on them from previous meals to feed Colonel Rundles's command for a month. It clung to the plates and the forks and would either have to be eaten around or along with the current fare.

I thought of Tippi's perfectly clean and organized kitchen as I watched the Indian girl working around the fire. I suppose it was the sack of oatmeal cookies stashed away in my saddlebags that brought that vision to mind. Enough had happened today to make even them look downright delectable. I was hungry, just not hungry enough to break bread with these characters.

Afterward, the aroma of their coffee made abstinence unbearable, and I was not offered any of that either.

In the twilight, with full bellies, they stretched out around the fire and talked about the day just past. They spoke of gold and silver and Indians, and throughout the fabric of their ramblings my name kept popping up like an errant thread.

There was some disagreement among them on the manner in which I was to be dealt with. Kenshoo had gathered up all the dirty dishes into a galvanized tub. With some hesitation, she went to Carl and spoke to him too softly for me to hear.

"No!" Carl erupted, turning on her viciously.

Kenshoo retreated.

"If I've told you once, woman, I've told you five hundred times. We ain't got the water to waste on such foolishness! Jest scrape 'em off and let 'em be."

Kenshoo cowered from his hot glare and knelt down by the wash tub. The mixture of night shadows and dancing yellow flames animated a stymied expression.

I have painted portraits of Indian women many times over the past five or six years, and their strength and quiet resolve always came across well on canvas, but in Kenshoo I saw something different. Her eyes expressed a certain amount of helplessness. It was understandable, but yet there was something there, something that bothered me.

I thought about it for a while, then shelved the problem for the time being. Perhaps I was only empathizing—feeling the pain of her iron shackle chafing my ankle, experiencing in my own way her apprehension of a pregnancy coming to term and bringing a child into the world that these three men offered to her.

What could have brought her to them, or was it the other way around? And why the shackle and chain? Who was going to be the father?

"What the hell are you doing, woman?"

Carl leaped to his feet and in three long strides was standing over her.

Kenshoo looked up at him, eyes wide with terror. He stood over her, his fingers came together, and he swung out. She tumbled backward, stunned, and tried to push herself from the ground and fell back.

"You stupid bitch!" Carl directed the toe of his boot at her swollen abdomen.

Kenshoo saw it coming and rolled quickly, shielding her unborn child. The force of the kick went into her back. She cried out with pain.

I hadn't seen what had provoked Carl's wrath. One minute Kenshoo had been scouring the pans with sand, and then the next moment Carl was a raving maniac. I didn't bother to try to figure it out, and without thought to my tied hands or the rope that anchored me, I leaped forward.

But I came up short of rope and fell. Carl halted his attack on Kenshoo at that point and wheeled around.

"You want to get in this, too, mister?"

Two angry strides brought him above me. I rolled to one side and caught the force of his boot on the side.

It hurt, but I've been hit harder. Scrambling, I got to my feet only to discover the tether was too short for me to stand. Kneeling was the best I could do, and that put me at an excellent height for Carl to use his fists.

He employed them brazenly, but not with the skill of a fighter. Carl was a bully and not accustomed to being stood up against. He openly telegraphed his punches and I had no difficulty reading them as they came, rolling with them and avoiding any real serious injury. Still, it was no fun. After taking half a dozen poorly placed blows I feigned unconsciousness and toppled to the ground.

That seemed to satisfy his anger and with a parting stab of his toe, he strode back to Kenshoo.

The rage left him as swiftly as it had come, and I still had no notion what had caused the violent storm. Kenshoo was equally confused as she lay on the ground with wide, wary eyes. But the storm had passed. It had worn itself out against my chin, and a frighteningly easy calm came over Carl as he picked the iron skillet off the ground and shook the sand from it.

"It will ruin the pan, Kenshoo," he said unemotionally, setting it down with the other dirty dishes. "Scratchin' them clean with sand will ruin 'em, and I don't ever want to see you do it again. Just wipe 'em with a rag and leave 'em. Understand?"

She nodded her head and watched him return to his place by the fire.

The others hadn't seemed to notice the storm that had just blown through.

I decided it was safe enough to regain consciousness and with a groan that mostly was genuine, I pushed myself up and looked around as if in a daze.

"How you feeling?" Weevil asked, grinning.

"I hurt."

"'Tain't surprising."

I said, "How about a drink of water to wash the dust from my mouth?"

Weevil glanced at Carl.

"Go ahead, give him a drink."

He swung from one emotional extreme to the other. I wonder how long the beneficent side would last and if it was always like this after the rage had subsided.

Weevil said to Cary, "Git the man a drink o' water."

"Why me?"

"'Cause I'm telling you to."

The kid got to his feet reluctantly, dipped a water ladle into an open barrel, and carried it to me. He put it to my lips. Water trickled down my chin as I drank deeply, not sure when another drink would be coming. Tomorrow might prove to be a long, hot day.

"How does that taste, Mr. Gatelatch?" Cary rocked back on his haunches and studied me in that peculiar way of his.

"Good."

"You really paint pictures?" he asked suddenly.

"I really do."

"I ain't never met an artist before."

"Now you have."

"You don't look no different from anyone else."

Where do people get that idea from? I know many artists and a few writers, too, and not one of them would stand out in a crowd. Still, it seems almost a universal notion that if you make your living in the world of art you somehow have to look different. Perhaps I ought to wear a tam-o'-shanter and a gaudy silk scarf, and tuck paintbrushes behind my ears or clench them between my teeth. I suppose there should be paint stains all over my clothing too. After all, who ever heard of a neat artist? Come to think of it, maybe sloppiness is a genuine criterion for an artist. The disarray of my house compared to Tippi's neatly arranged clutter must certainly prove something.

Cary's eyes shifted off my face. He reached out and yanked at the corner of the envelope that had poked up out of my shirt pocket during Carl's battering.

"What's this?" he asked, bending toward the fire.

I was as curious as he. "It's my grocery list."

"Grocery list, huh?" He laughed. "Then how come it's addressed to Colonel William T. Hauser. Huh? He your grocer?" Cary snickered again.

"What you find there, boy?"

"Looks like a letter, Uncle Weevil."

"Bring it here."

Cary gave it to him. He turned it over, peered at the name scrawled across the front of it, and asked Cary to read it to him again. "It says: 'Colonel William T. Hauser.'" Weevil thought a moment. "Hauser? Ain't he the commandant over at Fort Avery?"

"He is," Carl said. "Open it up and read what's written there."

"That's government property," I said. Weevil chuckled as the paper ripped.

Well, I'd said the words I was supposed to. Not that I had the least fear that they would heed the warning, and nor was I certain I wanted them to. At least now I'd get an opportunity to hear what was so damned important that Rundles couldn't have sent it by regular courier.

Weevil fanned the paper open and squinted at it in the wavering firelight.

"Here, boy, read it to us."

Cary snapped the paper taut and leaned toward the fire.

"It says—ah… 'Dear Bill'"

"Dear Bill?" Weevil hooted. "That sounds pretty chummy to me."

"How is life up there in mountain country? Cooler, I should think, than what we are tolerating down here on the plains. It has been an oven here the last three weeks with no signs of rain, and it is getting hotter in other ways too. This morning one of the McClains rode into town looking for Able Gate. It was Ryan's brother, Barrister, and you know what kind of trouble he can be!!!

"Well, you and I and the U.S. Cavalry have too much invested in Abe to have him exposed to Barrister McClain. I have no doubt Abe could best the man, even on his worst day, but to do so, here, would ruin his cover which we've worked so hard to secure. He's too valuable an asset to lose just because Barrister is set on avenging his brother's death."

I appreciated the vote of confidence, but it did little to cool my rising temperature.

Cary paused in his reading and I sat there under the steady gaze of three pairs of eyes.

Cary cleared his throat and turned back to the paper in his hand:

"So, that's why I am sending him along with this letter to you, Bill. Abe would never leave town on my suggestion alone and I thought this the most expedient way to get him away from here for a few days. Just nod your head gravely as you read this and thank him for performing such a fine service, or whatever you think is best to keep his suspicions at bay. Abe is a clever man and I wouldn't want him to learn of this ruse. Keep him there with you a day or two, then send him back with a reply of some sort. I appreciate it.

"Hope Sarah and young William are all fine and perhaps we'll get a chance to come out and visit before you break camp for the winter. Irene has been hinting she'd like to see the mountains in the fall. The plains get awful tiresome sometimes.

"Take care and thanks again, Bill. Sincerely, Colonel Oliver Rundles, Commandant, Fort Evan Woods."

Cary folded the paper and looked across at me. The others were staring too. I shifted uncomfortably on the ground and discovered that Kenshoo had halted her stacking of dirty dishes and was watching me with open curiosity.

"Able Gate," Carl said finally. "We got us Able Gate tied up here!"

"Yeah," Weevil said with less enthusiasm. "But now that we got him, what we gonna do with him?"

"I don't know...yet," Carl said, tugging at his chin.

I had the uncomfortable feeling that he'd figure out something.

Cary circled me slowly and said, "He don't look so tough, now do he, Uncle Weevil?" I remembered similar words coming from Walt Teral's mouth about another gent who was indeed very tough.

"Don't get no foolish notions, boy," Weevil advised.

Cary hunkered down, grinning, and tossed a pebble that hit me in the center of the chest. He said, "Able Gate, well, what do you know! A big-name gunfighter right here in front of us. And it turns out he works in secret for the cavalry too. Won't that make for some interesting talk around the saloon the next time I ride into town."

Damn Oliver Rundles!

11

SOMETIME LATER that evening I discovered the source of the growing dung heap alongside their tent—that was as far as Kenshoo's chain would reach. I turned my head in embarrassment and disgust. Anger welled as my view narrowed at the men stretched out around the fire, making their plans.

I wasn't able to hear all their words, but those I did catch didn't sound encouraging. They had discussed and discarded several possible solutions to the problem I presented and were tossing back and forth yet another.

I waited until Kenshoo hobbled back into camp so as not to draw attention to her, then said, "Why do you keep her chained up?"

Weevil glanced up at me. "She'd run off if we didn't. Run back to her people, she would."

"Then let her go. She's not an animal to be chained."

"She's only a squaw," Carl said.

In the red glow of the embers I saw Kenshoo wince, but she remained otherwise unmoved by the conversation.

"With her people is where she belongs. She'll be needing their help soon."

Carl snorted. "You mean 'cause she's with child? Shoot, Gate, don't you know nothin'? Them Injun gals don't need no help. Not with that sort of thing. Nature takes good care of 'em when it comes to childbearing. They're like cows and horses. They jest drop 'em where they're standing, pick 'em up, dry 'em off, and keep on going."

Weevil and Cary laughed.

I strained against the ropes.

"Looky there, Carl," Cary said. "You went and made Mr. Able Gate mad."

"Oh, wouldn't want to stir the anger of the dangerous Able Gate."

I wasn't doing myself or Kenshoo any good. I eased back. The proper time would present itself, and when it did I'd be ready.

Their discussion eventually dissipated into scattered grunts and half-spoken phrases. The coals died back to an occasional red flicker at the urging of the cool and sporadic wind. They finally retired to their tents, Carl tugging Kenshoo after him into the nearer tent.

I huddled in the chill cussing myself for being so careless as to have ridden into their camp so completely unaware of the danger. I cussed Ollie Rundles too.

I thought of Mary Landers and wondered what she would do when I didn't show up for the dance. I thought of Walt Teral, but by that time I was all cussed out.

But I couldn't help being furious at the man who had sent me out on this wild-goose chase. It would all blow up in his face now, and for what? To get me out of town because of what might happen! What did happen was many times worse.

Rundles had done a good job of blowing my cover—the thing he feared, and now Cary had the evidence in writing—Colonel Oliver Rundles's writing. I couldn't help thinking Rundles was going to get what was coming to him; it was only too bad the price would include my hide if I couldn't figure a way out of this.

I moved near the stake. It was as thick as my forearm with the top crushed down and splintered where a heavy hammer had driven it into the ground. Kenshoo's chain was wrapped around it and fastened by several stout nails driven in halfway and hammered over. Impossible to remove without some sort of prying tool.

Soft snoring began from the farther tent and presently snoring started from Carl's place.

I backed up to the stake and began working the ropes against the bent nails. After an hour I had not managed to accomplish much more than to fray the heavy cords.

The chain moved. I glanced at Carl's tent. Kenshoo appeared at the door, looked briefly at me across the darkness that separated us, then limped around to the side of the tent.

I turned my head away. When I looked back a few minutes later she was standing at the farthest reaches of her chain and staring at something in the darkness.

Silhouetted against the slightly brighter night sky, she might have passed for a statue but for the frayed hem of her dress that moved under the urging of a slight breeze. Finally, after several minutes, her shoulders heaved once and her chin fell forward. She turned back and brushed a finger across her eyes.

"Kenshoo," I whispered.

She stopped, looked at me, and this time both hands wiped vigorously at her eyes.

"Come here."

Her head shook. She had not only herself but the baby inside her to protect.

"Cut me loose and I'll get you away from here."

She hesitated, then stepped back toward the tent shaking her head. I was only a maybe rescue whereas Carl posed a very real threat if he were to catch her aiding me. A very real and deadly threat.

I continued at the knot, stopping finally to consider my dilemma. Sometime during the night weariness overcame the penetrating chill and my growing discomfort.

A sound woke me. Weevil was up with the dawn and stretched himself out of the tent.

Sitting up, I said, "I've got to take a leak."

"That's your problem, Gate."

"It will be yours if I start messing the ground in the middle of your camp."

From what I had already seen I didn't think a little more mess would ever be noticed, but Weevil must have thought it would cause a problem. He rousted out Cary and shoved the shotgun into his hands. Then he untied the rope and marched me beyond the perimeter of the camp.

"Now, don't get a clever notion or nothing, Mr. Gate," Weevil warned, loosening my hands and stepping back out of my reach.

I rubbed my wrists and glanced at Cary. His face had lost its cocky confidence now that my hands were free. He clutched the shotgun to his shoulder as if someone were seriously contemplating taking the thing away from him.

Someone was, but that someone couldn't see any way to do it without catching a load of buckshot in the process.

I turned my back to them and noticed the nearby mound of overturned earth. It could only have been a few weeks old. New grass and weeds were beginning to push slender green blades above the black soil.

Its general size and shape were unmistakable. I remembered the argument between Weevil and Carl before Cary had arrived. Afterward, they escorted me back to camp and made certain I was securely retied to the stake.

Carl emerged from his tent a few minutes later and stopped to wrinkle his forehead at me. Then, with his thoughts unspoken, he swung the pick over his shoulder, grabbed up a coal oil lamp, and marched into the mine. "You go on with him," Weevil said.

"Don't you want me to stay and help you watch this feller, Uncle Weevil?"

"He ain't goin' nowheres, boy, now git to work. I'll give a holler when mornin' vittles are fixed."

Cary grabbed up a pick, a lantern, and a bucket, and with his head craned over his shoulder he stepped into the dark rectangle after Carl.

When he had gone I said, "How long you going to keep me tied up here?"

"'Til we decide what to do with you."

"And how long will that be?"

Weevil looked at me curiously. "You anxious to die or something, mister?"

"Or something."

He gathered together some wood and moved it by the fire pit.

"Who's buried over yonder?"

"'Tain't none o' your business."

Kenshoo chose that moment to stand out of the tent and brush futilely at the leather dress, but the dirt and the wrinkles were still there when she finished. Her glance around the camp paused briefly on me. She squared her shoulders and set about rebuilding the fire and filling the coffeepot.

In that instant I felt it again—that something about her wasn't ringing true. But the feeling passed so quickly I was left only with my doubts to ponder.

Coffee and breakfast smelled mighty good. After a day and a night without food, I was ready to eat off their thrice-used plates. A study of the texture and color of growing mold might have proved a profitable endeavor for a part-time artist. Fortunately, I was not given the opportunity.

Weevil called his partners from the mine shaft. They came into the daylight in the middle of a rapid-fire, hand-waving discussion that at first I mistook for a raging argument, but in a minute I recognized it for what it was.

They hauled Weevil aside and huddled down together. From the occasional glances and the long hard stares I figured they had finally determined what to do with me, and as they broke apart they seemed quite pleased with the solution.

They ate their breakfast cheerfully, and I had the uncomfortable feeling that I had suddenly grown hair all over my body and sprouted a tail. Just throw the monkey a banana. They stared like happy children in a zoo and somehow all their wide grins came across flashing dollar signs.

As they put their mornin' vittles aside I figured I'd take a chance and ask for a cup of coffee. The request was granted.

Surprise number one!

Surprise number two came when Kenshoo brought the cup to me and held it carefully to my mouth.

I looked at her and immediately forgot the coffee and just sat there staring.

Suddenly I knew what it was about this Indian girl that had disturbed me, what didn't feel right. My subconscious had picked it out immediately, but it took her getting right down in front of me, this close, for my conscious brain to pick it out too.

I stared at her, and then at them, and then back at her again.

Kenshoo had blue eyes!

12

THERE WERE other things too—obvious things now that I knew what to look for. Things that, for an artist who has painted Indian women before, should have leaped out and hit me between the eyes.

The texture of her skin.

The shape of her eyes.

Her hair, although oily and filthy, was not black at all but a rich brown and fine textured.

But she moved like an Indian, with an economy of motion that made every movement account for something. She let me take the cup between my lips at my own pace, not hurrying the hot liquid down my throat. When I finished she returned to the fire without having spoken a word.

Carl, Weevil, and Cary were busy finalizing their plans...plans I'd have given my best camel-hair brush to listen in on. They eventually came to some kind of agreement, and Cary moved off to his tent. When he appeared again it was with a jacket and a leather sack in hand.

Weevil was harnessing the horses to the wagon. Cary climbed aboard and took the reins.

"I'll be back in a few days," he said, turning an eye on me. "Make sure he's still here when we get back."

We?

"He'll be here, all right," Carl said. "You just be certain you get our price, and don't go telling him what we're adoing, neither."

"I'll do it right," Cary said, annoyed at having to be told the obvious. He snapped the reins and the wagon clattered out of camp.

Carl and Weevil stood there until the wagon was out of sight, then Carl shouldered the pick and went back to work.

Weevil leaned the shotgun against his tent and seemed happier than usual.

"Did you boys get it all worked out?"

"We sure did." Weevil grinned.

"I don't suppose it's any of my business?" I shifted on the ground searching for that elusive comfortable position. There was none.

"I don't mind atellin' you seeing as you're pretty much tied up here." He chuckled, stuck a finger up his nose with rewarding results. "We're gonna sell you."

"Sell me?"

"You heard right." Weevil had difficulty containing his delight to about the same degree as I had difficulty containing my confusion.

"Sell me to whom?"

He seemed surprised. "Why, to that Barrister McClain feller, that's who."

It was something I should have suspected, yet it caught me by surprise. I didn't know if I should laugh or offer Weevil my condolences. I said, "You sent Cary out to make a deal with Barrister McClain?"

"Yep."

"McClain will cut that boy up in little pieces as soon as look at him, especially if he tries to demand money out of him! Whatever made you think you could bargain with McClain?"

A fleeting look of concern reshaped Weevil's face. He shrugged it off and said, "We got something he wants. You. Cary says he overheard talk in town 'bout how you gunned down McClain's brother, Ryan. And that letter your colonel friend sent along sort of proves that McClain wants you pretty bad. I think he'll be willing to deal."

I said, "I think you better start making plans to bury your nephew."

Weevil stood up angrily. "And you best be making your own final plans, Mr. Able Gate! Cary will get along just fine."

I'd planted doubt-seeds in their neatly packaged plan, and that was good. I knew McClain's reputation better than most because of the work I did tracking down Ryan McClain, and I knew he took what he wanted. He wasn't accustomed to paying for things; not the broken glasses or the whiskey he was drinking at the Custer Saloon, and not for me either if Cary should have the misfortune of finding McClain and making the offer.

"We need more water," Kenshoo said. She was standing by the fire holding the blackened coffeepot.

"Git it yourself," Weevil said, glaring over his shoulder at her.

Kenshoo extended her arm with the pot dangling from her fingers. "If you want coffee you will have to get the water for me."

His sudden anger at me had clouded his thinking. He remembered whom he was talking to and, with an impatient glance at the chain about her ankle, he stomped back and snatched the coffeepot from her hand.

At the wooden water barrel he cussed, kicked it over, and watched the few remaining drops trickle away into the sand. He righted the barrel, grabbed up two buckets, and went out to fetch more water from wherever it was they supplied themselves. He stopped, thought a moment, then went back for the shotgun, then clutched it under his arm and stomped out of camp.

"Try not to upset them," Kenshoo warned softly, dragging the chain over the ground.

As I looked at her now, all I could see was a white woman dressed in Indian clothing. She spoke with an uncertainty common to people who have not used their native language for many years. She knew all the words, and how to arrange them properly, but they came out slow and deliberate and she clipped off their ends as if combining the peculiarities of another language with them.

"They can be quite evil when they want to be," she said, looking off in the direction Weevil had gone.

"How did you come to be here?"

Kenshoo peered out into space, frowned, and said, "My husband and I happened into their camp…much as you did. We did not expect trouble. They treated us friendly at first, told us of their mine and the wealth it contained. Then later, during the night, they shot my husband and took me. I resisted at first." She shuddered. "They can be very evil."

The major Indian conflicts had ended nearly a decade ago, soon after the defeat of Custer. Public outcry had sent soldiers to clean out the Indian problem and an uneasy but lasting peace had prevailed. It was not uncommon for Indians and white men to pass along the trail and continue on, each to his own destination. It would not be unrealistic for Kenshoo and her husband to pass by a white man's camp expecting no hostilities. "Where is your husband now?"

Kenshoo glanced over her shoulder past the squalid tent and the pieces of the puzzle came together. They had killed Kenshoo's husband because Carl bragged about the mine, then buried him in a shallow grave outside of camp and chained his pregnant wife to do their bidding.

"You are white," I said.

She looked startled. "I am of the Sioux tribe."

"Perhaps, but you weren't born Sioux."

An inner conflict that I could see she had wrestled with a time or two in the past showed in the look of perplexity on her face. She dismissed the old problem with a brief wave of her hand. "We have no time to talk," she said, glancing over her shoulder. She hesitated and looked back at me. "You said you would take me with you?"

"Yes."

She came to a decision then and said, "Tonight. When they sleep."

Kenshoo moved back to the fire, and a few moments later Weevil struggled into camp hauling two buckets of water and trying to keep the shotgun from slipping out from under his arm.

The water splashed into the barrel and he went back out for another run. Kenshoo busied herself at the fire, going out of her way not to take any notice of me.

I didn't know what she had in mind, so I tried not to make any plans contingent on what she might do. Still, it was impossible not to think about it, and that helped me keep from thinking about the sun glaring down on the open patch of ground where I was anchored.

By noon I asked for my hat. Kenshoo found it stuck in a bush where the wind had deposited it the previous night after Carl's temper and his fists had sent it flying.

They ate lunch and I decided it was about time they started offering the prisoner some, but they didn't feel the same. They were working under the premise that a hungry prisoner was a weakened prisoner and therefore a safer and easier-to-manage prisoner.

I managed to get a cup of water out of them. I figured that was doing pretty good considering what value Carl placed on his water supply.

The sun inched past its noonday high and began chipping away at the latter half of the day. Kenshoo did not say anything to me, and except for fetching my hat and bringing me a drink, she went about her activities as if I were not there. In the middle of the day she retreated to the shade of the tent, and I didn't see her again until the day was well spent.

Weevil hauled enough water to top off the barrel and then disappeared for a while. He came back with a load of wood bundled in his arms and dropped it all by the fire pit.

As the afternoon wore on, Weevil and Carl changed places. Weevil shouldered a pick and disappeared into the mine. Carl slung the shotgun under his arm and took a stroll around the perimeter of their camp, pausing at the picket line where my horse was tied.

He looked the animal over awhile then stood there peering down at my saddle where it had been tossed on the ground. He moved the animal to a place where grass still remained underfoot and brought it a bucket of Weevil's newly hauled water.

I had never felt envious of a horse before.

He came back and settled down in a spot of shade beside Weevil's tent and sipped a cup of water. We looked at each other awhile then I closed my eyes and tried not to think of the mid-afternoon heat.

I tried not to think about anything as they ate dinner—at least nothing that reminded me of food. It actually takes a man a long time to die from starvation, if he has water, which they were supplying me in small portions, but I was having a difficult time convincing my stomach of that.

A dark shade drew across the sky and the sun extinguished itself in a final burst of red that spread across the mountaintops as if somewhere beyond a munitions dump had exploded. I did a good job of thinking about other things—I had a lot of other things to think about—until they poured the coffee.

I watched them. Weevil glanced up at me and said, "Care for a cup?"

"Yes, I would."

"No!"

We looked at Carl.

"He gets no coffee," Carl said.

The beneficent phase had passed and Carl had taken a pendulum's course back to his same old grouchy self. In my mind I did some violent things to him, felt a little better for it, and requested instead some water.

Carl nodded his head. Weevil fetched it from the barrel and handed it to Kenshoo to administer.

I still had no idea what she had in mind, and she was not giving out secrets as she wordlessly put the dipper to my lips.

Later that evening I got a glimpse of what she was planning. From the food box she brought out a bottle of whiskey and showed it to Carl, asking what she ought to do with it.

"I'll take care of it," he said, his eyes gleaming.

Weevil moved over. "Ooowee, looky what Cary went and bought for us."

"The kid ain't all that bad after all," Carl said, working the cork out with his teeth.

They toasted Cary and went to work on the bottle. As the evening passed everyone got toasted…including me. I even got a cup of coffee later, nicely laced with whiskey.

Kenshoo stayed quietly in the background, her eyes seldom straying from them, and when they did it was only to view me.

By midnight the bottle lay empty upon the ground with Weevil asleep next to it, beside the warm ring of rocks that held the dying remains of their fire.

Carl grunted, rolled his head, and heaved himself shakily to his feet.

"Come on," he said. Speech had become an effort.

Kenshoo went inside the tent. Carl wobbled to the water barrel, drank about half of it, then turned and aimed for the tent. A minute, and several course corrections later, he arrived and ducked inside.

There came a muffled thud as something hit the ground. Carl had gone to bed.

13

COLD STEEL SLID between my wrists and the cords parted and fell away. I was free again. The rush of blood sent firebrands coursing through my hands to my fingertips. I rubbed the lifeless slabs of meat together.

Kenshoo rocked back on her haunches, taking her expression with her as her face receded into the darkness. Moonlight glinted off the long blade in her hand, and she sat there turning her head back and forth from me to the quiet tent.

"What now?" she whispered.

"Give me a minute to get some feeling back." I stood shakily and glanced down at the slumbering form by the nearly dead fire. Kenshoo joined me at my side.

"Where do they keep the key to that thing?"

She looked at the iron band about her ankle and the padlock that secured it to the chain.

"I do not know."

"Great."

"You promised to take me with you!"

"I'm not going to leave you."

She lifted her head and widened her blue eyes at me. In that moment I thought I caught a glimpse of someone else. I looked at her, startled, and knew I was mistaken. Still, I found myself studying the line of her mouth, the shape of her nose.

She looked at the chain around her ankle. "How?"

"I don't know—yet." Feeling was beginning to rear its ugly head. My hands burned and I thought briefly of the water barrel, deciding perhaps that would not be a smart move. It would pass in due time.

"Where did you get that?"

She glanced at the knife in her hand. "From there." She nodded at the cooking supplies.

"Careless of them to let it out for you."

"I have not caused them any trouble. At first they were careful about everything, but lately they have had other things to think about. I keep it in the bottom of a large pot which is not used. I put the smaller pots on top."

"Out of sight, out of mind."

She looked at me curiously and then a smile touched her lips as she seemed to recall something. "Yes, that is how it goes. I remember now—but it has been so long."

"How long?"

Kenshoo shrugged her shoulders. "I do not know. I remember nothing except in dreams I do not understand, or when I see something and know I have seen it before. But I know not when or where."

Weevil stirred, moved on the ground, and settled back to even breathing.

"We better figure a way to get you out of here." I motioned for her to sit on the ground and wait while I did some exploring.

The heaps of junk scattered about made moving around quietly impossible. I tripped across a coil of rusty chain and threw an apprehensive glance at Weevil. He snorted in his sleep and shifted upon the ground. I waited for regular breathing to return, then crawled into his and Cary's tent and began rummaging through the mess there.

Blankets and pillows and a wooden crate littered the floor—the floor was but the hard-packed earth beneath it. I hit my head on a lantern suspended from the cross pole, then knocked over a box set back in the corner. The lamp was still squeaking softly up on the pole when I huddled down in the darkness and waited for the quiet to return. I wasn't being very good at being quiet, but my hands still refused to work properly even though the fire was subsiding and feeling was returning.

I discovered my holster and gun was in the box I'd kicked over. I fumbled it around my waist and tightened the buckle with fingers that seemed too large.

I felt around inside the box, and among the bedding and clothes strewn about, but found nothing that resembled a key. I shook out my hands thinking that even if I did feel a key I'd not recognize its shape.

I unearthed a carton of matches, considered striking one, but decided against such open advertisement of my presence and shoved them into my pocket instead. I continued through Weevil's tent, trying to put a name to the many items my fingers ran across, and in the end came away with nothing useful. I paused there a moment to think out the situation. The key had to be with Carl. Well, I was armed now. I didn't see any major problem in going over there, putting a gun to his head, and asking for it.

Actually, the notion sounded pretty good, and I wondered, as I started for the door of Weevil's tent, why I had bothered looking for it at all once I had my revolver back. Sure, the old hands weren't working quite right yet, but they were good enough to do what needed to be done.

It was a simple enough plan and I saw no flaws in it as I stuck my head out of the tent. Then something hard smashed into the back of my skull. A million stars exploded into my brain, and as I rolled over onto the ground I glimpsed a pair of steel eyes peering over me…and then only blackness.

14

WHEN I SAW THE STARS AGAIN, the real ones in the sky, those two steel eyes were still peering down at me. I groaned. The eyes wavered. Weevil took a step backward and jerked the shotgun in his hands.

"Git on over there," he said.

Kenshoo had a hand clasped over her mouth and blood was working its way through her fingers. I rose unsteadily and went to her. The shotgun behind me urged me on, and my empty holster, twisted around, flopped in front of me.

Carl ground his knuckles into the palm of his left hand. "Sit down!" he said.

I joined Kenshoo on the ground beside the smoldering embers of last night's fire. Weevil held the scattergun on me, squinting over the barrels as he had that first time I stumbled into their camp.

"What we gonna do with them, Carl?"

"I don't know." Carl tucked his shirt tail into his pants and pulled the suspenders over his shoulders. "I'm for shootin' 'em both right there where they sit."

Kenshoo's eyes widened.

"I don't know 'bout that, Carl. What'll we tell that McClain feller when he comes to collect his goods?"

"He'll have to settle for a corpse."

"He might want ours in the bargain if'n he thinks we double-crossed him."

I could see the seeds of doubt I'd planted in Weevil's brain taking sprout, but that didn't matter to Carl. He was itching for blood—our blood—and he'd worry about the cost to himself later. My gun was in his hand and he looked at it, thought it over, and decided a dead Able Gate was safer than a disappointed Barrister McClain.

"Kill him, Weevil. Kill 'em both."

"You sure, Carl?"

I slid my hand into my pocket, grasped the box of lucifers, and tossed it into the embers at the moment Carl glared at Weevil.

"If you ain't got the stomach for it then stand clear." My gun came up in his hand.

"It ain't them I'm worried about. What are we gonna tell McClain? He ain't a forgiving man, from what I hear."

"Let me worry about explaining it to McClain. I'm flat tired of looking after him, and she's worthless too, all fat like that. Shit, there ain't a good screw left in her."

Weevil looked unconvinced. He lowered the shotgun and said, "Well, if you want them dead then I guess you'll have to do it, Carl. Killing a man straight out don't bother me none, but killing that woman, well, I guess you're right. I ain't got the stomach for it."

"Then stand aside." Carl drew back on the hammer of my pistol. I sucked in a breath, ready to move, trying to judge the pressure he was putting on the trigger. Then the box of lucifers flared among the coals. The flash drew Carl's eyes, and in that instant I leaped for the shotgun in Weevil's hands.

I hit him hard. The wind went out of him and we tumbled to the ground, me locked onto the shotgun determined it was going to take someone meatier than Weevil to wrench it from my grasp.

I heard the thunder of the pistol, saw the muzzle flash out the corner of my eye, and wondered, distantly, where the bullet had gone. It hadn't hit me, and once I had that figured out I feared for Kenshoo, but I had my hands too full to do anything about it.

I rolled to my back hauling Weevil with me and saw, in a fleeting glimpse, Carl trying to follow us with the gun. Then Weevil and I were nose to nose. Weevil gritted his teeth and I heaved up a knee, sending him somersaulting overhead, still grasping the neck of the shotgun.

The pistol steadied on my unprotected side. I followed Weevil in a backward roll as it exploded again and kicked up a spray of dirt from the spot I'd occupied a split second before.

The gun followed. Carl was red with rage.

I winced as the pistol barked a third time.

Weevil cried out and the shotgun went limp in his hands. I yanked it free and swung it around, but as my finger went for the forward trigger Kenshoo leaped in front of it. I heaved the gun up as the roar and flash ripped a hole in the night sky.

Carl had been concentrating full on me. He never saw the blade arched high above his chest, or the glint of the cold steel in the moonlight.

He cried out as it plunged deep into his heart. Cried out once and looked with shock as Kenshoo pulled the blade out and brought it down again. The gun fell to the ground and so did he with the knife handle stuck to his chest. Kenshoo dove after it and proceeded to thrust the blade deep time after time.

I lowered the hammer on the second barrel of the shotgun and set it aside. Weevil wasn't moving and my ears were ringing like the squeal of brakes from a downhill locomotive coming to a halt. Kenshoo was hammering away at Carl. She swiveled around with a wide, unseeing craziness in her eyes when I took her by the shoulders.

"That's enough, Kenshoo," I said, "that's enough, he's dead."

It took a moment for my words to make sense to her. When they finally did reach down into that portion of her brain that had retained a semblance of sanity, she trembled and the knife dropped onto Carl's lifeless chest. I took her into my arms and held her as the terror left her body in a series of convulsive tremors.

"Drink this."

"Coffee?"

"It will make you feel better."

"I don't think so."

"It can't hurt."

She accepted the logic of that and sipped. She made a face and handed the cup back to me. "How can you drink that?"

"You acquire the taste."

"It is not something I am ready to acquire."

"Have it your way." I drank hers and attacked my own. Maybe Kenshoo didn't need it, but I sure did.

"I've never killed anyone before," she said after a while.

"It's not easy."

"Yet...yet I do not feel remorse. Shouldn't I?"

"I suppose it depends. As far as Carl goes, well, I'm not surprised. He didn't treat you very well."

"He murdered my husband." She turned her head back toward the fire I'd built up from the bed of embers then glanced at the empty whiskey bottle by its rock enclosure.

"I could use some of that."

"It's not good for you."

"I know. It drives Indians crazy. I never did understand why," she said. "It never bothered me."

"You're not Indian."

"I'm Sioux."

"In name only."

Kenshoo looked at her hands then rubbed them on her deerskin dress as if doing so would wipe away her heritage.

"I never knew the white world." The yellow firelight danced off her pale skin.

"You must've known it well enough to learn to speak the language."

"Perhaps, but I do not remember."

"Except in dreams."

"I must have been very young."

"Six or seven?"

"I don't know. Listen, could we get this thing off of me?"

Her English was improving with leaps and bounds. All it takes is practice, I mused. Living with Carl didn't provide much of that. He did all the talking and she had an opportunity to do a lot of listening.

"Sure. I'll see if I can find a key."

I had dragged the bodies back behind the tents where they were out of sight. I checked Carl first and came away empty-handed. Same with Weevil.

Inside the tent I struck a match. It flared against the tent pole and set the untrimmed lantern wick afire. I lowered the glass and began to tear apart the clutter of Carl's tent. It was every bit as thick as that in Weevil's and Cary's. The stench of filthy clothes filled the confined air and made breathing painful.

I found Carl's pouch, heavy with the profits of his work. Perhaps legally gained, perhaps not. How many other travelers had he and Weevil waylaid? I didn't think Carl had been one to quibble over keeping ill-gotten gold. In any case, he'd not be needing it now. I tucked the pouch into my pocket where it bulged uncomfortably.

I carried the lantern over to Weevil's tent and went through it more carefully this time, came away with two more pouches but no key.

"Any ideas?" I asked Kenshoo when I'd run out of places to look.

"I never saw it after he put it in his pocket."

"The pocket of his pants?"

She paused to think. "No, it was a jacket he was wearing. He put the key in the pocket of a jacket."

"I didn't see a jacket."

"There must be one somewhere," she said. "He has worn it from time to time."

I went back through the tents, holding my breath, and came out stumped. I tried to think where Carl would keep a jacket. There was only one place left. Kenshoo continued a far-off gaze at the flames and did not look at me when I passed by. I was curious about the mine anyway. Holding the lamp high in front of me, I entered the hole.

It wasn't much of a mine as far as mines went, and my experience with them was not great. The walls were uneven with hardly enough room between them for a man to stand let alone swing a pick. I noted with some apprehension the total lack of shoring and bracing and imagined more than actually heard a steady rain of fine pebbles from the roof that arched a foot above my head.

The shaft ended abruptly two dozen feet back. Upon an upended wooden box I balanced the lantern and looked around. Leaning against the end of the tunnel was Carl's pickax. Two dented buckets sat beside it. A spike driven into the rock wall served as a hanger for a canteen.

I lifted the box, looked underneath, and found nothing. Frowning, I turned back and started out.

Then something caught my eye. I held the lamp out. On the wall, hanging from a second spike, was Carl's coat.

15

THE DAWN BROUGHT new hope for Kenshoo. She seemed to relish her newfound freedom and spent a considerable time wandering around beyond the limits of the chain that now lay like a dead serpent upon the ground. I tugged the cinch snug and filled my saddlebags with provisions from their food box. The recovered letter from Rundles was tucked safely in my pocket, and I tried not to think about what I was going to do with it when I returned— or with him. He was my commanding officer, but I didn't think that would stop me from pursuing whatever course I decided was appropriate between here and there.

I finished saddling up and looked around for Kenshoo. I found her standing by the grave out back, the bloodied knife clutched in her hand, her back to me. I waited as she said her farewell to her husband by herself. She knelt down and placed the knife atop the mounded dirt, then turned, surprised to see me standing there.

"Are you ready to go?" I asked.

"Yes."

She passed Carl and Weevil's bodies without a glance, stopped by the horse, and looked solemnly around the camp.

"I'll help you up," I said.

"I can walk."

"Maybe, but you should give that ankle a rest."

She saw the wisdom in that and agreed to be helped into the saddle.

"Where are we going?" she asked, looking down at me.

"Back to Fort Evan Woods." I gathered up the reins.

"I want to go back to my people."

"The cavalry will see that you are reunited with them. In the meantime I don't intend to go wandering around out here looking for your people."

"Very well," she said.

We turned our backs to the mountains and headed off into the rising sun. The day wore on uneventfully, and we rested at noon beneath a grove of cottonwoods beside a meandering stream.

Kenshoo climbed stiffly out of the saddle and pushed her hands into the small of her back as she went down to the water. She washed her face and drank deeply, and when she returned it was with renewed vigor. I studied her face, thinking that, in some ways, it was a familiar face, and trying to figure out just what it was that made it so.

"Hungry?" I asked, scraping together sticks into a pile and putting a match to them.

"Yes," she said, lowering herself awkwardly to the ground and resting against a tree.

"I'll have some beans heated in a few minutes. There is some bread too. We'll rest here awhile."

Kenshoo leaned her head back against the tree trunk and closed her eyes while I cut open the lid on a can of Van Camps and put it among the flames. I carried two plates and a pair of spoons down to the water and scrubbed them clean. Probably the first time the metal had seen daylight in months, I mused as I rinsed them out in the clear water.

The beans were boiling when I returned. I plucked the can from the coals with a couple sticks and doled out equal portions.

"Lunch is ready."

Kenshoo's eyes opened heavily. She straightened up and took the plate.

"We even have clean plates to eat from."

Kenshoo only grunted as she attacked the beans and sopped up the juice with the chunk of bread.

"Some more?"

She nodded her head and I refilled her plate.

"You're eating for two," I observed.

Kenshoo gave me a curious look.

"You and the baby."

She looked down at herself.

"It's just an expression."

She looked even more confused.

"Forget it."

She returned her attention to the food.

"When are you due?" I asked after a while.

"Due?"

"The baby. How soon will it be born?"

She understood and glanced up at the sky, then made two sweeping passes with her arm.

"Two months?"

"Yes. Two months."

"Not long."

She smiled suddenly. "No, not long," she said, and sat there smiling for a long, contented moment, then remembered the food and had at it again.

I broke down the fire when we'd finished and was adjusting the cinch when Kenshoo came up behind me.

"Thank you," she said when I looked around at her.

"You're welcome." Her unwavering gaze remained on me a long, silent moment. I said, "Time to get moving again."

Kenshoo offered no objection when I helped her into the saddle.

"Feel better?"

She frowned and said, "It took the edge off."

"Edge off? That's not an Indian expression."

"No, it is not." she said, somewhat embarrassed. "I do that sometimes, say things without knowing where I heard them."

"Something from the past?"

"I suppose so," she said thoughtfully.

"But you are still hungry."

She smiled for only the second time. "Like you said, I'm eating for two now."

"I think I've something in those saddlebags that might help." I unbuckled the flap and removed the brown bag. Most of the cookies had dissolved into chunks that were slowly grinding themselves into cookie dust, but I found one that had managed to survive the trip without suffering much more damage than a ragged edge.

"An oatmeal cookie!" she cried with a sudden sparkle of childlike glee in her eyes. "What's wrong?" she asked as my hand came to a halt just out of reach of hers.

"How did you know that?"

"Know what?"

"That this was an oatmeal cookie."

"Why...I don't know. It just came out." Kenshoo was as surprised as I was.

I studied the wrinkle of concern across her forehead, measured the width of her mouth compressed now into a tight line, and compared it to another face I knew so well. A knot constructed itself out of the cords of my intestines. I knew what I was thinking was unlikely, but not impossible. I gave her the cookie and she tasted it experimentally. A smile replaced the frown, a smile that also matched the face in my memory.

"It even tastes like an oatmeal cookie!" Kenshoo said joyously.

"Not surprising," I commented, keeping my suspicions to myself.

She looked at me and said, "Funny I should know that."

"Something out of your past, no doubt."

"No doubt," she answered more somberly. That night we made camp on a wide expanse of Montana plains that bobbed away in all directions like gentle, green waves. In the distance the saw-tooth line of mountains we had come from had melted down almost to the line of the horizon.

Over the fire that flickered in the dying light the rest of our food bubbled in its can, and a pot of coffee sat off to the side perking happily on the cherry-red coals, filling the air with a delicious aroma. I'd kept back some jerked beef and of course the crumbs in my brown paper bag for breakfast in the morning. I figured by noon we'd be at the fort where Rundles could damn well feed us and try to talk his way out of the crumpled piece of paper I was carrying back to him.

My anger on that point had subsided somewhat as I had had a full day to watch the happy expression on Kenshoo's face. Although I'd been nearly killed, some good had come of it, and I conceded that through his conniving to get me out of town and away from Barrister McClain, Ollie Rundles had had some small part in her rescue.

With our hunger slain and our stomachs content, we stretched out on the ground and roamed about the private world of our thoughts for a little while. Kenshoo claimed the saddle and tried to make herself comfortable against it, curling up in a blanket we had brought along. But in her condition, there were very few comfortable postures, and I doubted even a feather bed could accommodate her very long before a shift in position would be required.

After a while I locked the door on my reminiscing and looked at Kenshoo, determined to try to discover the answers to the questions that had been forming all day.

"Kenshoo?"

"Huh?"

She may have been dozing. She turned heavily on the saddle and looked at me.

"How much of your past do you remember?"

"I told you. I remember nothing."

"You must have some memories."

"No, none that I am aware of. Except for the occasional lapses. Words that sometimes come out, words I don't recall having ever heard before, but I know, somehow, what they mean. Or perhaps an unfamiliar odor will make me feel happy or sad, and I do not know why. Maybe a face or a scene will make me wonder where I have seen it before, but I'm not able to find an answer."

"Then you don't remember when you came to live with the Sioux?"

"Only vaguely. Those memories are all jumbled up in my brain. I seem to recall there was a lot going on at a certain point in my life. I seem to recall there was a lot of sadness, and then I was taken in by one of the older women of the lodge. My mother. She had other children, much older than me, so she had a lot of time to spend with me alone. I was happy then, sort of like a hole in my life had been filled. After that I was sad less often until I was not sad at all. What happened before, I just can't remember. I must have been very young. All my memories seem to start from the time my mother took me in."

"And what about the dreams?"

Kenshoo shrugged and shifted her position on the ground. "They never make any sense. Mostly they are filled with violence, and in them I'm running away from someplace or someone, only I never seem to get anywhere. I run, but I cannot run away."

"Is that all?"

"Sometimes I'll see faces. A man's face, a woman's face—" Kenshoo paused then smiled. "And in some of the dreams I'm riding a horse, but it is a very strange horse. It does not go anywhere. Like when I'm fleeing and not getting anywhere. It just stays in one place and goes back and forth, but whenever I awake from that dream I find I am happy. That does sound strange, doesn't it, Mr. Gate?"

"What color is the horse that goes nowhere?" I asked, recalling the tinplate on Tippi's mantel.

She thought then said, "I believe it is white, with black spots all over it."

My skin was tingling. It was all but impossible, but there were just too many coincidences to ignore.

"Kenshoo," I said, leaning forward. "Does the name Tippi mean anything to you?"

She thought and her head shook slowly. "No, should it?"

I tried again. "How about the name Sara Ann Mullroy?"

She thought longer on this but her reply was the same.

I threw out half a dozen other words that might spark a memory, but it appeared that those flames were truly dead, if indeed they ever existed in her memory to begin with. Perhaps I had jumped to a wrong conclusion. Tippi had said time and time again that Sara Ann had been killed in an Indian attack. Why should I doubt it?

But Kenshoo had taken the questions to heart. Now as I turned to refill my cup from the pot among the coals, she sat there in deep contemplation.

My back was to her when she whispered it, as if struggling to pull the words, fighting and clawing, from some dark recess where they had retired, fat and comfortable all these long years.

She spoke the single phrase I had failed to mention in all my questioning, and when she did the coffeepot jerked up in my hand and coffee sizzled on the coals.

I wheeled back to her. "What did you say?"

My intensity startled her.

She gazed at me and repeated the words. Then, as if not quite sure what she had said to bring such a reaction from me,

103

she said it again—just to be certain she had it right. "The Sergeant?"

16

"SARA ANN MULLROY?" she asked.

"Uh-huh."

"Are you sure, Mr. Gate?"

"I don't think there is much doubt. Your name is—was— Sara Ann Mullroy. Your mother's name is Tippi, and your father, well, Tippi always referred to him as 'the Sergeant.'"

She stared straight ahead and repeated the name softly under her breath. Beneath her, the horse continued its steady plodding with me alongside carrying the reins. I'd gone through the whole story with her the night before, and I don't think either one of us got much sleep. After our fire burned low and the conversation developed long gaps, I laid there watching the stars, wondering how Tippi would take the news that the daughter she'd thought was dead was still alive and well, and about to make her a grandmother. Sometime later I drifted off to sleep. When I awoke, Kenshoo/Sara Ann was already up urging the coals into productive flames.

"I remembered something else," she said as I shook off a deathlike sleep and joined her by the fire. "There was a picture. I remembered it last night before I fell asleep, and then I saw it in a dream. The picture was of two people, a woman in a long white dress standing next to a man, a big man—"

"That was their wedding picture," I said. "Tippi still has it. It sits on the mantel."

She was suddenly concerned. "Will Tippi—I mean, my mother—will she want to see me? I was only a little child when I was taken. Really, I'm more Indian than white."

I grinned at her. "She'll be ecstatic." "Ecstatic?"

"She'll love you until you can hardly breathe. Don't worry about her not wanting to see you."

Throughout the morning she remained wrapped up with her thoughts, a smile and a frown battling for dominance upon her face, and now, with the sun approaching noon, she began asking questions once more.

"Tell me about my mother again."

I kicked at a rock on the trail and shrugged my shoulders. "I think I've told you most everything. Tippi is a sweet old lady who sort of looks after all the younger folks in town like they were her own children. That's because she didn't have any children of her own—until now."

"She sounds nice."

"She is."

"What about my father?"

"I never knew the Sergeant very well. We'd met only briefly a few months before he was killed, and I only saw him a time or two before his death. Actually, he died not more than a dozen feet from me. I hadn't met Tippi at that time, of course. That happened some years later, but I remembered him speak of her, and of course, Tippi always spoke of him. And occasionally of you, although that memory was painful."

"How did he die?" Kenshoo asked.

I had hoped she wouldn't ask that, but this was no time to be keeping back something that had to come out.

I said, "He died at the battle of the Little Big Horn. A Sioux arrow."

Kenshoo sat back in the saddle and the horse instinctively came to a halt.

"It's no fault of yours, or even your people, Kenshoo," I said. "It was during a bad time. Those days are over."

"But you don't understand. I was there. I was in the encampment. My husband was a young warrior. He fought Yellow Hair—"

"It's unlikely he was the one," I said, frowning.

"But he could have been," she said.

"And that's something we'll never know. Don't go making extra problems for yourself. Enough of them will come along of their own."

She fell into a deep silence and remained quiet until the fort came in sight several hours later.

"There it is," I said, stopping on the crest of a hill. "Fort Evan Woods."

She studied it with apprehension digging deep furrows into her face.

"Don't worry, Kenshoo, you'll make out fine."

"All my life I've been taught to fear the cavalry and not to trust the white man. I'm...I'm not sure I want to go down there."

"Your mother is down there."

"A woman I don't know," she said. "Back there"—she looked over her shoulder—"I have a mother I do know."

"Well, we have to go to the fort." I started forward.

"Gate!" She grabbed at the reins. "I've got to think this through. Please give me some time."

"Listen," I said gently, "no matter how you were raised, you are still white, and down there is a mother you don't remember, but she remembers you and she still loves you. Down there is where you belong."

"Are you so sure I belong with the white man just because white blood flows through my body? I'm Sioux! I was raised Sioux. I think like the Sioux. If I am white, it is in name only."

"I can't just let you turn around and ride away."

"Why not?"

That was a good question.

"Because I'll be alone? I've been alone before."

"No, that's not it."

"Maybe it's because I'm going to have a baby soon?" She laughed bitterly. "Carl was right, you know. We Indians are more animal than human. We just drop them where we are standing, pick them up and dry them off, and keep on going."

"Carl didn't have the brains to fill a thimble."

"It's what the whites think of Indians, isn't it?"

"Not all whites."

"But down there there will be some. At least back home I'm accepted as one of their own."

"And you'll be accepted here too."

Her jaw took a firm set. "I don't want to go."

"You have to."

"Why?"

"Your mother is down there."

"She thinks I'm dead. We can leave it at that."

"And how about you?"

The sternness in her face faltered. "I'll forget what you told me. There is a woman down there I don't know and you tell me she's my mother. Maybe it will be easier on both of us if I do ride away without ever meeting. You don't have to tell her."

"You're right, I don't have to tell her, but I still have to take you down to the fort."

"But why?" she implored for the third time.

"How far do you think you can walk on an ankle swollen the size of a grapefruit, and seven months pregnant—and having to hunt water and food?"

"I can take this horse."

"This horse is government property. I can't go giving it away."

She stiffened. "And is that what I will become? Government property?"

"Of course not."

"You said the cavalry would take me back to my people. What do you think the chances of that will be?"

"No one can force you to stay if you don't want to."

She gave a short laugh. "With a father who was a sergeant in the cavalry and a mother who lives in the same town, what chance will I ever have of leaving again?"

There was some truth in what she said. "All right," I said, "there is no way to hide the fact that you are white, but we don't have to tell them who you are."

"What do you mean?"

"I mean, you're an adult woman, and if you want to return to the Indians no one can stop you. I won't tell them you are Sara Ann Mullroy and I won't tell Tippi either. I'll leave that decision up to you, Kenshoo. If you decide you want to leave, I'll do nothing to stand in your way."

"You would do this for me?"

"I would."

Kenshoo thought it over and, with a certain amount of resolve shaping itself in her face, she said, "All right, Mr. Gate, I will go down there with you."

"Well, thank you."

"Not a word as to who I am?"

"Not a word."

She nodded and the long, knotted hair moved along her back. "Then let's go, I'm getting behind on my eating for two."

We came straight into the main gates despite Rundles's desire that I always use the side entrance, and then after dark if at all possible. But I had enough of Rundles's games. I'd been square with him, and he'd dealt me a stacked hand. There'd be some settling of accounts before things went back to the way they had been.

We made quite a display, a pregnant woman astride my horse, me wearing a gun and lacking the spectacles and suit they had all come to know me by.

"Abernathy?" a young lieutenant by the name of Roberts said, stepping close for a good look.

"Hello, Mark. The colonel in?"

"Yes, he is. What you got there?"

I ignored him and angled across the parade ground. Ollie Rundles stepped out the door and watched us from the front porch. He looked at Kenshoo as I wrapped the reins over the hitching post then turned a worried face at me.

"Hello, Abe. I'm glad you're back. Come on in."

Something was terribly wrong.

"What happened?"

He only shook his head and stepped back into the darkness of his office. I helped Kenshoo to the ground and we followed him.

"Close the door," he said, settling wearily behind his desk. He looked at Kenshoo, glanced questioningly at me. "Never mind, it can wait."

"What is it, Ollie?" I'd forgotten the letter in my pocket. All at once I knew. "It's McClain, isn't it?"

He drew a deep breath and looked up at me. "I thought my men could handle him. I misjudged the man, and perhaps my own men too."

"Anybody hurt?"

Rundles nodded and his lips came together into an angry knot. "I lost four men. Three civilians were killed, half the town burned…and something else, Abe."

A chill ran up my spine at his intonation.

"Maybe you better sit down."

"Just say it straight out."

"Okay. McClain took Mary Landers with him. I know how you feel about her."

I'd started for the door. "Wait a minute," he said.

I turned with my hand on the handle.

"One other thing."

"What?"

"Tippi Mullroy. You know how she is about our boys. When she saw what was happening she put herself between McClain and one of my men. She was shot. She's badly injured."

Kenshoo swayed on her feet. I reached out and caught her before she reached the floor.

17

"WHAT'S WRONG with her?"

"You mean besides the obvious?"

He gave me an impatient look.

I said, "She is seven months pregnant and she hasn't eaten for almost a day."

"I'll have something brought up from the mess hall," Rundles said, turning for the door.

I helped Kenshoo into the chair he vacated. "Are you all right?"

She looked at me with dilated eyes, color slowly pinkening her cheeks again. "Yes…I'm fine now."

Rundles came back in, shutting the door behind him. "I've sent for a tray of food. How is she?"

"Better, now. She's had a rough time of it."

He bent closer to look at her. "My God. She's white!"

"I had a similar reaction."

"Is this something you'd care to tell me about?"

"It's too involved to go into it here. Tell me about McClain, and Mary and Tippi." He cleared his throat, poured water from a crystal pitcher into a crystal glass, and offered it to Kenshoo.

"Thank you."

"You're welcome, my dear." He glanced at me and we walked around to the front of the desk. The features of his face settled into a severe mask.

"Randy Linger never did come back," Ollie said, frowning, "and I'm not sure that boy didn't have more sense than most folks in town has given him credit for. McClain hung around for another couple days, drinking whiskey like those damned beasts the government pushed on us a few years back drank water."

"Ships of the desert," I said.

"We know why they're called that. The dozen or so we had down in Arizona used to run our cistern down to dry gravel in about three days. They should have left them damn, foul animals in Arabia or wherever the hell they got them from."

"Get back on the subject."

He cleared his throat. "Of course. I put a couple men in town just to keep an eye on him, like I promised you. Then about two days ago this kid comes into town aboard a buckboard, looking for McClain. He wasn't hard to find. By that time the saloon was starting to look threadbare and the hitching rail outside was broken. No one had bothered to sweep up the window glass on the front sidewalk either, since no one was venturing anywhere near the saloon. Even Clyde Woolman had made a discreet exit, leaving the place to McClain, who seemed hellbent on draining every cask Clyde owned."

"The kid with the buckboard would have been Cary," I said.

Kenshoo looked up from the glass of water. "I never learned his name," Rundles said. "He asked where he could find McClain and someone pointed him in the right direction and that was all. He halted the wagon in front of the Custer Saloon and went inside."

"What happened then?"

"A few minutes later it sounded as if an earthquake had begun to rumble under the Custer. Everything breakable began to do so, including, we speculate, one of the lamps, because shortly McClain and the kid stepped out into the street with flames licking their heels from inside."

Rundles paused, "I don't know what transpired in there between the kid and him, but whatever it was, McClain was killing-mad. He pulled his gun and began shooting at people. It was at that point my men stepped in.

"And?" I said when he fell into an introspective silence.

"It becomes a little unclear at this point. So much was happening. The upshot of the whole thing was that my men were not a match for McClain even though the man was rocking drunk and hadn't slept in two days, except on his feet at the bar."

"How did Tippi get hurt?"

He grimaced. "You know how Tippi feels about boys in blue. How she mothers them like they were her own."

"Yes."

"She was there when the shooting started, shopping, I think, she and Mary Landers. Young Barry Crenshaw was the first of my men to go down. Tippi saw it and went to his aid, scolding and shaking a fist at McClain. At least that's what I've been told by several witnesses."

"And McClain shot her?"

Rundles nodded his head. "Like she'd been a rabid coyote raiding his chicken coop." Kenshoo was listening to it all. Her face drained of color and her eyes went wide. I glanced back at Rundles.

"But she's still alive?"

"Tippi is at Doc's house and he isn't saying what her chances are. You know Doc; when he keeps his mouth shut it's not going well."

I turned and stared out the window at the parade ground. I couldn't help thinking none of this would have happened if Rundles hadn't tried to be clever getting me out of town, but he didn't need that thrown into his face now. He was already burdening himself with the responsibility. When I looked back Kenshoo was just sitting there holding the glass of water, staring at something no one else could see. There wasn't anything I could do to help Tippi now, but I could stop McClain.

"Okay," I said, bringing my eyes back to his. "Men got killed, Tippi is hurt. What have you done about it?"

He winced as if my words had been a knife in his back. "As soon as I got the word I mounted a patrol. McClain and the kid had left—"

"And Mary?"

"Apparently that was the kid's idea. She had gone to Tippi's side. The kid pulled her away and hauled her to the buckboard. McClain was still filling the street with lead and no one made an effort to stop him. Mary struggled, of course, and the kid hit her. I heard various versions of it, but the consensus was that she was unconscious when he lifted her into the back of the buckboard."

I rammed my fist into my palm with a sharp crack that sounded like a pistol shot in the suddenly quiet office. A knock sounded at the door. Rundles opened it, took the tray of food, and set it in front of Kenshoo.

"Here you go, my dear," he said.

She picked at a slab of roasted beef and poked her finger at the baked potato. There was silverware on the tray, which she completely ignored.

Rundles looked back at me and said, "By the time I got word of the incident an hour had already passed. The Custer was on fire and Merel's Pharmacy was burning too. They were busy trying to prevent the fire from spreading so naturally we weren't informed immediately. When word reached us I rode into town, saw what had happened, and hurried over to Doc's house where the wounded had been moved to." He paused, then said, "By the time we got organized and moving, well, something like three hours had passed. They had gotten a big jump on us and were moving fast."

"They couldn't have gone very fast in that buckboard, not the shape those animals were in.

He looked at me, surprised, and said, "You seem to know quite a bit about this."

"I do, but I haven't got time to tell you all about it now."

Rundles looked at Kenshoo then back at me. "It should make interesting listening," he said.

"Very," I said. "So, where are they now?" Rundles pursed his lips then shook his head and stepped to the window, putting his back to me. "We came across the buckboard about an hour out of town. The animals were grazing in some tall grass." He paused and turned slowly back, showing a tortured face, heavy with a burden of guilt almost too great to bear.

"At first we didn't see the bodies, then one of my men found the little girl. Her mother and father were nearby…both dead. The little girl lived long enough to tell us about the two men who had ridden up to their carriage, pulled out their guns, and shot them without a word.

"They took the carriage the child and her parents were driving. Two horses, and well-conditioned, judging by the distance they put between my men."

"So, where are they now, Ollie?"

"We almost had them when they crossed into Canada."

"And you didn't go after them?" But his hands were tied. The border was as far as he could venture without getting himself tangled in a bureaucratic rat's nest. "Never mind," I said.

"That's why we keep you around," he came back angrily, then remembered we were not alone in the room and glanced at Kenshoo.

I gave a short laugh. "It's too late to worry about her, Ollie. She already knows enough to blow our cover wide open if she wanted to," I said, trying to maintain an even voice, but my anger of the last several days was again rising to the surface. "If you hadn't sent me off on a wild-goose chase none of this would have happened."

Rundles narrowed an eye at me. It widened when I dug the wrinkled paper from my pocket and handed it to him. He unfolded it with a decided lack of enthusiasm.

"She read this?"

"No, it was read to her—to the both of us, by that kid that just crossed the Canadian border with Barrister McClain."

Rundles turned mechanically back to the window. The hard line of his mouth reflected in the glass. "You're going to have to go after them, Abe," he said.

"I know." I took Kenshoo's hand and started for the door. She came willingly with the remains of her roast beef clutched in her other hand.

"Where are you taking her?"

"I have to find her someplace to stay."

"I can put her up here at the post." Kenshoo glanced quickly at me and her fingers dug into my hand.

"I think she'll be happier in town, Ollie." He understood and nodded his head. "Maybe you ought to leave your gun."

"It seems a little late to be trying to patch things together, Ollie."

"Maybe," he said, resuming his position of authority. "Just the same…"

I unbuckled the gun belt and dropped it on his desk. There was still the matter of rank, and he was my commanding officer. "I'll be back," I said.

18

ONCE BURNED, TWICE SHY...or so the saying goes.

I reined to a stop at the first indication of smoke in the air, thinking this was all too familiar. In the darkness that had overtaken and had occupied the land for the last hour, I studied the uncertain terrain. The thin, cold moon and the stars didn't help much. High clouds absorbed most of the light before it reached the ocean of grass that stretched away darkly before me.

Ahead, in the trough of a ravine, a light flickered. I left the horse ground-tied and made my way for it on foot, taking to the ground the last dozen feet, snakelike, to the rim of the ravine.

A small campfire crackled; its light danced across the ground, illuminating the front of the man sitting there. His back was to me, darkly silhouetted against the fire. He poked the flames with a stick and pulled out a firebrand, then touched it to a cigarette between his lips. The odor in the air changed. A horse was tied some distance away, its saddle now serving as a back rest for the man below.

Elbowing away from the ravine, I regained my feet and circled several hundred feet to enter the ravine out of sight and sound of the fellow below. I hadn't seen a face, yet I knew for certain the man was neither Barrister McClain nor Cary. Those two would be farther over the border according to the information Rundles had supplied me before I'd left the post. Still, there was something strangely familiar about the man below, in the shape of his back, in the way he sat brooding into the fire, and I meant to find out what it was.

I started down the ravine recalling my conversation with Rundles before I'd left. "We had to turn back at the border," he had said when I returned from taking Kenshoo into town. As he moved to the map on the wall behind his desk, I was thinking about the uncertainty in Kenshoo's eyes when I put her into the care of Mort and Berniece Weaver.

"We'll take proper care of the girl," Berniece said, draping a protective arm over Kenshoo's shoulder.

Kenshoo stiffened beneath the older woman's touch, but remained standing there in the Weavers' parlor looking at me with searching blue eyes.

"I'll be back," I told her. She knew that was a promise I might not be able to keep considering McClain's reputation. I told the Weavers nothing of her past, only that she was a white girl taken by the Indians as a child. The Weavers didn't ask any more.

"Are you certain you know what you're doing, Abernathy?" Mort said, working his lips into a worried frown.

"Someone has to go after her. The cavalry can't, not legally."

"But you can't go up against someone like Barrister McClain," he said.

I grinned. "It's surprising what a man can do when he has to."

He tried to mirror my smile but I could tell when he extended his big, rough, blacksmith's hand, he was saying good-bye in what he figured was a permanent way.

"Then good luck," he said, and Berniece pulled Kenshoo closer to her side.

I left her there and headed up to Doc's house. His wife greeted me at the door and seemed to know intuitively why I had come.

"Oh, Abernathy," she said, pulling the door wide for me. "I'm so glad you're here." She paused and looked at my clothing. The wrinkles of her forehead deepened.

"I just came in off the prairie," I said in answer to the question I saw coming, and stepped inside. She closed the door.

"Tippi is over this way." She led me down the narrow hallway, into a door.

Doc Bidley looked up when the door opened. "Hello, Abernathy."

I stood over the bed. Tippi's powder-white face seemed even paler than usual. Her eyelids lay like wrinkled rose petals over her closed eyes. One arm was out of the covers, across her chest, which moved imperceptibly with each breath.

"How is she doing?" I discovered I was whispering, as if I was in the presence of death.

Bidley wagged his head and stripped the stethoscope from around his neck. He thrust a hand into his pocket and said, "There is nothing more I can do for her."

"What's her chances?"

"Not good, but it's up to her now. If the will to live is strong, well, she has a fighting chance. If she decides to let go, it won't take long."

"Damn," I said softly. "Has she regained consciousness?"

"She was alert for a little while, but mostly she sleeps."

Mrs. Bidley said, "We were hoping you'd show up, Abernathy. Tippi thinks highly of you. Perhaps if you were here, by her side when she wakes, it would give her encouragement."

"I'm not going to be able to stay," I said. They looked at me.

"Someone has to go after Mary."

"Not you!" Bidley exclaimed.

"I have to."

"But McClain will kill you."

"He'll try."

"Now, don't go off halfcocked," Bidley said. "We all feel for Mary, but it's foolish to go out and get yourself killed. There has got to be a better way to rescue the unfortunate girl than sacrificing good men to Barrister McClain."

Edna Bidley agreed and added, "There is progress right now to form a posse and go after them."

"Randy Linger is back in town?"

"He returned this afternoon," she said. "He's out looking for men right now, and I suspect your help will be welcomed."

"Do you know how to use a gun?" Doc Bidley asked.

"A little."

"Then you join up with them, if you must go," Edna said. "But I wish you would consider staying, for Tippi's sake."

"I wish I could."

They didn't press the point. I stayed with Tippi a few minutes longer then allowed Edna to show me to the door.

"You take care of yourself, Abernathy," she said when she let me out.

I assured her I would and walked down the street to Randy Linger's office. The door was locked. A note tacked there informed anyone who was interested that he'd be back shortly. I didn't have the time to wait for him and I suspected Rundles would have as much information, if not more, than Randy had had time to acquire. I rode back to the post, collected my gun, and had Rundles send out to the mess hall for something to fill the empty hole in my stomach.

Rundles paused, studied the wall map, then tapped it with a finger and said, "They crossed into Canada at this point. My guess is that they are heading for either Regway or East Poplar. Of course, there are a half-dozen other places between that don't show up on our maps: Waseca, Govan, Lacy Springs, Hardy, and a few others I can't recall. They could be heading for any one of those places, or anywhere else in Saskatchewan for that matter."

"Thanks for limiting my area of search," I said.

He frowned. "Sorry, Abe, but it's all I have."

I stood, snatching my hat off the top of his desk. "Then I better get onto their trail before it turns colder than a Canadian winter."

He saw me out the door. "Take care, Abe, and good luck."

"Thanks." I swung up onto the horse and reached back into the saddlebags. "I almost forgot about these," I said, handing him the three pouches of gold I'd taken from Carl and Weevil's tent. "Would you see that they're kept in a safe place until I get back? And if I don't, see that Kenshoo gets them."

"Kenshoo?" He weighed the heavy pouches in his hand.

"She deserves them," I said, and didn't offer any further explanation.

"I'll see that she gets them—if you don't come back."

"Appreciate it." I left by way of the main gate with Rundles standing on the porch in front of his office frowning. Any anonymity I might have had on the post before this happened was surely gone, and he knew it. Years of carefully constructed stories and nice knitted covers were now flung wide and the truth was known. One thing was certain: I would never be able to live here as I used to.

Maybe that was for the best. Maybe I'd used up my time here. There were other places the cavalry could set me up—if they chose to, if I chose to pursue this line of work after this was over.

I put the dilemma out of my mind; thinking about it now served no useful purpose, and there was the more immediate problem before me. Rundles had pointed me in the right direction and I had no problem following the wide trail the cavalry had beat into the ground pursuing McClain and Cary to the Canadian border.

I rode most of the night and stopped a few hours before dawn to sleep. In the morning hot coffee and hardtack made up my breakfast. Lunch was taken in the saddle. There were too many miles and not enough hours to waste any on eating.

It was somewhere around nightfall when I crossed the border. The trail stopped abruptly where the cavalry had turned back. Suddenly all that was left were the tracks of the carriage they had stolen with its two animals and a third horse ridden by McClain.

Darkness made following them difficult, but the carriage cut a wide trail through the grass and I was in no hurry now. They were safely into Canada and feeling secure. They'd slow their pace, maybe lay over for a day or two somewhere, and then I'd have them.

It was an hour later that I realized a fourth horse had joined up with them...or so it appeared.

I worked my way down to the bottom of the ravine and drew my revolver. A twig snapped beneath my boot and I paused to allow the sound to pass into the night. Then I continued along the sandy bottom, avoiding the bramble that grew up along the sides that tried to bar my way. Progress went at a snail's pace, but the man by the campfire wasn't going anywhere for the rest of the night, and anyway, I'd already adopted a patient, go-easy attitude.

The ravine widened up and I stepped into the open, still outside the ring of light the little fire cast. In profile, I was struck again by the feeling that I knew this man. When I stepped up alongside him and put the gun at his head, I was certain.

He heaved around at the sound of the hammer, startled at seeing me standing there.

His mouth dropped and his eyes popped. Then they narrowed at me and he began to breathe again.

"Abernathy!"

"Evening, Walt," I said, stepping into the light.

Able Gate

19

"WHAT THE HELL are you doing out here, Abernathy?" he said, still shaken at the sight of my six-shooter pointing at him.

"Probably the same as you're up to."

"McClain?"

"Uh-huh."

"You can't go up against a man like McClain, Abernathy." His words broke off and his eyes narrowed as if suddenly seeing me in a new light. "You ain't never worn a gun before...and your clothes? Why are you dressed like a...a cowboy? Where's that funny hat you always wear, and your spectacles?"

"I left them behind," I said, pushing my gun back into its holster.

"And you can see?"

"Pretty good."

Walt was confused. "But why do you wear them specs if'n you can see without 'em?" Then all at once the answer occurred to him. He cranked his mouth shut and his eyes expanded. "Wait a minute," he said, spacing out the words.

"Abernathy Gatelatch…Able—" He looked up at me. "Gate?"

I glanced at the coffeepot by the fire.

"Could you spare some of that?"

"Huh?"

"Coffee. I could sure use a cup of it."

He shook himself from his open-mouthed stupor and said, "Oh—oh, yeah," and he scrambled for the pot. "You really are Able Gate?" he said, then answered himself. "Of course you are! Why else would McClain know where to come looking for you? Able Gate! My God, who would have thought you to be a gunfighter!"

"Thanks," I said, taking the cup.

"You're gonna take on McClain?"

"I'm going to bring Mary back," I said. "If McClain gets in my way I'll deal with him."

"I'm going after him too," Walt said.

"I figured as much. How long have you been on their trail?"

"Almost three days. I came up right behind the cavalry, and when they turned back I just kept on going. I didn't guess there was no law keeping me from crossing over."

I lowered the coffee cup. "You've been following him for two days and this is all farther you've gotten?"

His face slackened and he looked away from me. "Well, I didn't want to get too close…At least not without some plan."

I laughed. "You've got more sense than I gave you credit for, Walt."

His eyes flashed up angrily, but he said nothing.

"Well," I said, "have you got one yet?"

He shook his head.

"Neither do I," I said. "I suppose the first thing to do is to find them."

"Well, I know where they are, Ab—ernathy. I mean—"

"Abernathy will do just fine," I said. "Where are they?"

"They're about five miles north of here," he said, regaining some enthusiasm, "in a little place called Lacy Springs. I was there—yesterday. I followed them into town then wandered over to the saloon where everyone was talking about Barrister McClain being back and how he'd wired somewhere for some kinfolk of his to meet him there. He's going to lay over for a few days then head back down into the States, him and a brother or cousin or something. That was when I figured I'd best fall back a few miles and think this thing through."

"That was yesterday?"

"Uh-huh. Yesterday afternoon."

"Then he's still alone."

"Maybe, but it seemed he had a lot of friends in Lacy Springs."

"Every man needs a safe port to come home to. This might be his."

"Then I think it's probably not a healthy place to be," he said thoughtfully.

"Probably not," I agreed, "and it certainly isn't going to get any healthier as more McClains start to arrive. Not for me and not for Mary either." I drained the cup and tapped grinds from the bottom of it. "Thanks for the coffee, Walt."

"Where you going?" he asked as I started up the incline.

"Lacy Springs."

"Now?"

"I'd like to get there before too many McClains begin to show up."

Walt scrambled to his feet. "I'm going with you."

The trouble with taking on a partner is looking out for his skin as well as your own, and Walt Teral would not be my first, or even my fifth, choice if I was given the luxury of making such a choice. I didn't need a headstrong and impulsive partner, nor did I want to be the one responsible for getting him killed. I was inclined to tell Walt I preferred to deal with the situation alone, but after rethinking the odds, an extra gun made the picture take on a rosier hue, if going from black to dark gray could by any stretch of the word be considered rosier.

"You sure?"

"Yes," he said instantly.

"All right. Put out that fire and saddle up. I'll be waiting for you on top."

I resumed the climb when he said, "Abernathy—I mean Able—"

I wheeled back. He was waging a sort of war internally that made itself known by the way he stammered and groped for the proper words.

"I...I guess I just wanted to say I was sorry for the way I acted the other night at the Custer. I mean, what I said about you...and about Mary. I was drunk and I was a little obnoxious." His hand moved to his chin and he grinned, embarrassed. "You sure do pack a wallop in that fist of yours, Mr. Gate, and I sure did deserve it."

"Forget it, Walt. And what's this mister stuff? Mr. Gate was my father. My name is Able, or Abernathy if you feel more comfortable using that one. It makes no difference to me." And as I started back up the incline I realized that it really didn't matter anymore, not as it did years ago when I first assumed the name in a moment of creative lapse. In many ways I'd grown comfortable in Abernathy's secure and unencumbered world. A world where the only dangers he had to deal with were the edge of a palette knife or the pointed handle of a paintbrush.

20

FROM THE ROAD Lacy Springs was indistinguishable from a hundred other one-lane towns that have sprung up, like wildflowers in May, all over southern Canada and northern Montana. And like wildflowers, most of them were destined to die and run away with the wind.

Walt rocked back in his saddle and pointed. "There it is."

"Where's the saloon?"

"That little building off to the right."

The squat, one-story shack sat next to a taller two-story structure of considerably larger dimensions. Both buildings showed light through their windows. The rest of the town was mostly dark. Only a few horses were tied up outside the saloon.

"Doesn't seem to be much going on," he said.

I opened my watch and tilted it toward the faint moonlight. "It's almost ten o'clock."

We started down the road again and I discovered that Lacy Springs had something that most wildflower-towns did not: a railroad. We crossed the tracks at the edge of town and came up the quiet street. Buildings moved in on either side of us, mostly dark, but a few showing a faint glow behind curtained windows.

I reined in in front of the saloon and studied the shambled affair. It was a poor excuse for a building, but then, drinking men never did need much of an excuse to tip back a bottle or sing a song. Tonight there wasn't any singing, and hardly any bottle tipping.

"Want to go in and take a look?" Walt said, swinging a leg off his animal.

"Not yet."

He stopped and straightened himself back into the saddle.

"Let's take a peek around Lacy Springs first. I'm sort of interested to see if it has a depot, or if the train just passes by."

"Why?"

I shrugged my shoulders. "I guess I just like trains."

There was a depot, and trains did stop, but not regularly, as was indicated by the schedule stuck up in a darkened window. According to the chalk markings, a freight train was due in at seven-ten in the morning. It wasn't scheduled to stop. I wondered how well the Canadian Pacific Railroad kept to its schedules as I turned away and followed a narrow lane down to some warehouses. Two flatcars sat on a siding in the weeds and the shadows alongside of one of the warehouses.

GRUMBLY'S MINING SUPPLIES AND TOOLS.

Walt glanced at the sign painted across the warehouse and said, "What do you suppose folks here do for a living, Abernathy?"

I grinned. "Haven't the faintest idea. Did you notice the name of that saloon?"

"No."

"The Glory Hole."

"You don't suppose folks in Lacy Springs have any interest in mining, do you?"

"The thought never crossed my mind," I said. We retraced our steps to the broader main street. The board

132

sidewalk on either side was built a good three feet above the road level with steps running down to the street on each corner, and every inch of space beneath the sidewalk was taken up with firewood stacked and ready for the winter.

We passed a Miners Mercantile and the boarded-up windows of an old BX stage stop. Up the only side street was the darkened bulk of a church, set well back from the town, and I wondered if that was an indication of the nature of Lacy Springs. If Barrister McClain thought of Lacy Springs as a safe refuge, I could see why the church would want to distance itself from it.

We came back to the saloon without finding a hotel in town. Standing beside the Glory Hole rose the tallest building in Lacy Springs. At first I mistook it for the hotel, but a moment of observation and listening assured me that what was going on inside there was not something any decent hotel would permit.

We tied up at the rail and walked around to the corner where rough-sawn steps brought us to the boardwalk.

Walt glanced through the dirty window. "It isn't very crowded."

"Just as well," I said. "Let me do the talking."

"What are you going to do?" he asked, trying unsuccessfully to hide his apprehension.

"We're going to go inside, buy a drink, and ask where we can find McClain."

"You can't just walk in there and tell them you're looking for McClain! My God, you'll have the whole town to fight!"

"I've got you to back me up," I said.

"That isn't even funny and you know it."

"You're right, it isn't. But if we are going to find McClain and Mary before too many of his kinfolk start to show up, we don't have time to tiptoe around in the dark looking in all the murky corners for them. The fastest way is to have him come to us, and that's what I intend to do. If you want to back out, Walt, I'll understand."

"No, I don't want to back out," he said, looking worried. "It's just that I didn't expect to go and announce openly what we were up to."

I said, "We'll have one drink. I repeat, one drink. We need to be sober. When McClain shows up you keep strictly out of it."

Walt nodded his head. "What do you want me to do?"

"I want you to sort of melt into the woodwork. I do not want you to draw attention to yourself. In fact, if you aren't wearing a gun, it might be better."

"No gun!" He caught himself and glanced through the dingy pane of glass to assure himself no one heard his outburst. "Are you crazy, Abernathy?"

"I've been accused of it, but I don't think so."

"What good can I do you if'n I'm not wearing a gun?"

"Plenty. I didn't say I wanted you to be unarmed, only that I didn't want you to openly wear your weapon."

"I don't follow?"

"Give me your gun belt."

He hesitated then unbuckled the belt and handed it over. I withdrew the gun, checked the loads, and handed it back to him. "Put it in back, under your belt, and make sure your vest covers what is left."

He tucked it into the small of his back and adjusted the vest.

"Turn around. Good. If you remember to stand straight no one will know you're armed."

"Fine. So, what's the point?"

"The point is, when I'm facing McClain, I want to know there is a friendly gun at my back keeping an eye on the crowd. If you're unarmed, and if you keep quietly to yourself, chances are when McClain arrives they will forget you're there. All eyes will be on me. At that point I don't want you to be watching me or McClain. I want you to be watching the crowd. Got that?"

He nodded his head and glanced through the dingy piece of glass set into the door. "I don't see him in there, Abernathy."

"Here, put your holster over your saddle." He hurried down the steps and when he returned we stepped inside. Instantly the murmurings ceased and half a dozen pairs of eyes turned toward us. There was a fire in the stove, which took the edge off the chilled air and made me realize how cold the night had become. Floorboards creaked and sagged beneath our feet.

"Whiskey for my friend and me," I said, sliding a coin across the bar.

"That money ain't no good here, mister," the bartender said. "I only take Canadian, or gold."

I fished around in my pocket and came out with a twenty-dollar piece. "Smallest I have."

"I can't change it," he said. "Too big." Behind us a chair scuffed on the floor and footsteps came up. "I'll buy these gentlemen a drink, Harold."

"Sure thing, Mr. Brasher," he said.

Walt and I turned.

"The name is Ben Brasher," he said, studying us with a cigar stuck between his teeth, puffing like a locomotive. "You boys are new in town. If you're planning to stay in Canada any length of time, I suggest you run over to St. Ives where they have a bank that can change your currency."

Our drinks came. I said, "Thanks for the advice, Mr. Brasher, and for the drinks. But we'll not be staying in Canada all that long."

"Up from the States on business?"

"I guess you could call it that," I said, tasting the drink. "I hear Barrister McClain is in town and I understand he's looking for me.

A sudden electricity seemed to flow through the saloon, polarizing the faces there.

Brasher's smile faltered. "I'm afraid I didn't catch your name."

"It's Gate. Able Gate, and I'd appreciate someone telling McClain that I'm waiting for him."

A man sitting by the door hopped up as if on cue and ran outside.

Brasher said, "We can wait at my table. McClain will probably be along directly."

I figured that Brasher was prone to understatements and accepted his offer.

We went to his table. Chairs scraped and men moved aside. Walt, I noted in a sideways glance, was not at all happy with the situation.

21

WAITING FOR BARRISTER MCCLAIN in the Glory Hole Saloon was a little like spending time in a goldfish bowl. Walt did a fair job of draining his whiskey glass and Ben Brasher did his best to make small talk, but he was finding it difficult, spending most of the time looking over his shoulder at the door.

Sometime later the man who had hurried out returned, sliding back into his chair. The bartender tossed a log into the stove and began to undo the neat stack of glasses behind the bar, putting them away under the bar. He moved the bottles out of sight too, in a practiced manner that made me think having his place broken apart was a regular occurrence.

Walt wiped perspiration from his forehead and returned his hat to his head. He had had a change of mind concerning McClain since that evening in the Custer Saloon.

Brasher asked if we wanted another drink.

"No, thank you," I said, noting in a glance that another drink was exactly what Walt wanted.

After a moment Brasher said, "You're the man that killed Ryan McClain a few months back."

"That's right."

"Barrister was hot over that."

"Ryan didn't give me a choice."

Brasher nodded his head. "It don't surprise me, knowing Ryan, but that doesn't swing much weight as far as the McClains are concerned. They're a hot-blooded clan and they stick together like tallow in December. They got that from their father's side, I reckon. The just plain meanness they got from their mother."

A chair scraped back upon the floor and a man in a dirty slicker and a wrinkled black hat stopped by our table. He was a tall, fence post of a man with a weather-carved face that resembled a large walnut. Black, bushy eyebrows nearly obscured his eyes, and in the uncertain light it was impossible to tell much about his face. He put himself between the hanging lamp and us.

"So, you're Able Gate," he said after a few moments of pondering. His hand moved back, sweeping aside the slicker, coming to rest on the butt of a pistol there.

A grin parted the walnut shell and he said, "Don't get jumpy. I'm not going to step in on Barrister's game. Just wanted to get a good look at you."

"I wasn't," I said, trying to recall where I'd seen that face before.

"I figured you for a bigger man," he said.

Then I had him pegged. I said, "And I figured you for a smarter man, Scott."

His grin faltered. "You know me?"

"Uh-huh. Scott Grindell. You were a buddy of Ryan McClain's." His grin faltered again and disappeared as my Colt came up from under the table where it had been pointing somewhere between his gut and his heart. I said, "A smart man wouldn't have moved for his gun like you did."

His hand slowly left its resting place and the slicker fell back at his side. "I've never seen you before."

"But I've seen you. You were with Ryan in Miles City. You rode out three days before Ryan made the mistake of drawing down on someone better than he. I suspect if you had stayed on you'd be dead too, Scott," I said, feeling the nervous strain grow in Walt as he fidgeted in his chair. Well, I'd given Walt someone in particular to keep an eye on now, someone I figured would step in and give McClain a hand if he had a chance. I hoped he remembered what I had told him.

"I'm going to see you off to hell today, Mr. Able Gate."

I holstered my gun. "Then you'll have to stand in line, Mr. Grindell, because someone else has prior claim." I nodded toward the door. I'd seen his dark form move on the boardwalk in front of the dingy windows, saw him pause and narrow an eye through the glass, and now the door crashed inward with a bang and Barrister McClain filled the door frame with his bulk.

Scott Grindell sprang back, startled. His face eased into a smile, seeing McClain standing there like a deformed bear. Grindell looked back at me and said, "So long, Mr. Able Gate. Tell the devil hello for me and that he won't be seeing me for a while."

Men moved out of the way and chairs scraped across the floor. Ben Brasher stood and said, "Well, it's been nice to have met you, Mr. Gate." He joined the mass exodus. I nodded at Walt and he became part of the gathering in the far corner of the saloon.

There was twenty feet of empty floor between Barrister McClain and me. He stopped just inside the door and fixed his dark eyes on me. His frock coat hung down to his boots and looked like he'd just collected it off the street after an Independence Day parade. The flat-brimmed hat was pulled down low on his head, encircled with a hat band of braided hair and raccoon paws. A black leather vest was buttoned up over a red shirt, and below the vest a Mexican silver buckle shone in the poor light.

"I know you," he said finally, his voice a rumble from deep inside.

"The Custer Saloon," I said. "Six days ago."

He grunted and nodded his head. "I didn't expect you to show up here."

"You took something with you that I want back."

"The girl?"

"That's right."

A slow smile spread across his unlovely face. It shaped itself into an ugly sneer and he said, "I'm going to keep that one awhile, leastways till I tire of her."

"And then there's the matter of a sweet old lady you gunned down as you were leaving town. She's a friend of mine," I said, stepping out from behind the table.

The crowd shifted in exactly the same direction until a wall prevented the tide from receding any farther.

McClain's left hand moved the coat away from the cross-draw rig he wore. Some men are deadly fast wearing their gun in that manner. McClain must have been one of them or his reputation wouldn't have grown. But then, I've never heard of him going against anyone but drunks, cowboys, or Mormon drovers. You can build a reputation on just plain meanness and keep those men who are really truly dangerous from even trying. I wouldn't want to dismiss him in such a cavalier fashion, though, as we faced each other, sizing each other up.

"It pains me to learn she's still alive, Gate," he said. "But that's not important. What's important is Ryan. You killed him, and for that I'm going to have your life."

"Your brother deserved what he got," I said, keeping my eyes on his eyes and trying not to think about the movement I sensed in the crowd behind me. I'd stationed Walt there to take care of those problems, and I put that flank of attack out of mind as McClain's eyes narrowed in response to my words.

I said, "Where is the girl now?"

A man stepped into the saloon, saw in a glance what was happening, and turned on his heels and hurried out.

"In the street, with the kid," he said, but his mind was already thinking ahead to his next move. His hand quivered tensely six inches from the Remington.

"Then let's get this over with, McClain," I said. I felt strangely at ease now as I held my view on his darkening eyes.

A silence deeper than death settled all around us.

McClain blinked. His gun came out and fired.

The bullet ripped a furrow in the wood between my feet, and a wide look of shock and surprise came across his face as he looked at me and then staggered back against the door frame.

He put a hand to his chest and it came away red. Rage replaced the shock and he drew back the hammer of his gun.

I fired again.

McClain spun around and went to his knees. He came about and fired. His bullet went wide and he was back up on his feet, cocking that damned Remington again.

I remembered Clarance Wimble's words that night in the Custer Saloon. "'The point is, that fellow at the bar has so much of the devil in him that you could shoot him three times and he'd never feel it—it wouldn't stop him from plugging you before he died.'" Clarance hadn't been far off the mark.

"Let it go," I said, but McClain wasn't listening. His gun came up and I shot him a third time. He slipped on his own blood, scrambled to his knees and stood up, rearing back like a grizzly bear.

Having no luck shooting me, he wheeled and threw the gun at my head with more force than I'd thought he had left inside him. He was bleeding from three places and madder than a wet cat.

I ducked and caught the glint of light off the long blade that appeared in his hand.

"Bastard!" he said, lumbering forward.

I knocked him back a step with my fourth bullet, but he straightened and lurched again. I fired my fifth shot and with an empty gun in my hand leaped out from under his plunging knife and grabbed up a chair. Whirling around, I shattered the chair against McClain's broad back and was left holding a handful of broken wood.

He went to the floor. I plucked up a second chair and held it above my head, wondering if this wasn't a bad dream come true, and wondering also how much furniture I was going to have to turn into kindling wood before he had had enough. McClain didn't move right away. I stood there with the chair poised and my heavy breathing burning my lungs.

His bulk shifted on the floor; there was a lot of red spreading out from under him. With a grunt, he heaved himself up and sat there looking at me through wide, glazed eyes. The hilt of his knife was stuck to his chest and he blinked down at it, touched it just to be sure what he was seeing was true, and looked up at me. The confusion left his eyes suddenly and a blind rage replaced it. He struggled to his knees, grabbed a nearby chair for support, and tried to stand.

He slipped on the blood. He came to rest on his knees, looked up at me with his hand still locked onto the chair, and died like that.

I let out a breath and set the chair down.

Behind me a gunshot rang out. I spun around. Scott Grindell stepped out of the crowd with his gun in hand. He had a look of surprise on his face as he turned his head over his shoulder. He took another step, holding himself strangely erect, then the gun fell to the floor, and a moment later so did he.

The men there moved apart leaving Walt standing with the still-smoking gun in his hand.

At the door a face peered inside. The young man behind it looked at McClain, looked at me, looked suddenly pale and terrified and, in a single bound, sprang out the door and leaped off the boardwalk onto the street.

Cary!

I plucked my gun from off the floor and dove after him.

22

HE SPRANG ABOARD the buggy and snapped the reins. I leaped from the boardwalk and yanked the Springfield from its scabbard, snapping it to my shoulder. On the seat beside him, Mary was having difficulty holding on. Maybe that was because her hands had been tied to the back of the seat. The carriage wheeled around a corner with a spray of dust and was gone.

Footsteps pounded the boardwalk behind me. Walt said, "Was that Mary?"

"It was," I said, lowering the rifle.

Behind Walt rose the sounds of men coming to grips with what had happened. More than mild amazement colored their voices and a growing anger was beginning to ripple through them. If McClain or Grindell really had any friends inside the Glory Hole Saloon, this would be a good time to be leaving, before the swell of anger became a tidal wave of hostile guns.

Inside the saloon someone said, "Well, are we gonna just let them two walk away after what they done?"

There immediately followed the sounds of disputation, rapidly working its way toward an end I did not care to stick around to see. I dug out the box of .45-55 shells from my saddlebags and tossed Walt his holster.

145

Men flooded out the door. I swung the Springfield on them and drew back the hammer. "Any of you boys figure you have a disagreement with us?" I said.

They piled together in the doorway and no one among them felt any great need to say anything one way or the other. The tunnel bore of the .45-55 lent a great urgency to choosing their next actions carefully.

"You killed McClain," someone shouted from the knot of men stuck in the door.

"And Grindell too," another said.

"They got friends here," the first voice said. I picked him out from the crowd. A stocky fellow with red hair and a tattered hat pulled down low over his eyes elbowed his way to the front. The men there seemed anxious to give up their front-row position to him.

I shifted the muzzle of the rifle. "You have something to say, mister?"

The man with the red beard stopped short and eyed the rifle. "Maybe you got the drop on us now, Gate, but don't go getting your hopes up too high. You ain't gonna ride out of Lacy Springs no way 'cept belly up in the back of a buckboard." His eyes shifted.

I turned in time to see the shadow move across the rooftop on the other side of the street. A pistol barked and fire stabbed out into the dark. I swung the rifle toward the spit of fire and in my mind's eye saw a swinging skillet hanging from a length of rawhide. The Springfield bellowed like a mountain howitzer and the figure lurched backward into the shadows. A gun skittered across the shingles, followed by a heavier sound and a thump.

When I turned back Walt was keeping our main problem at bay. "What do you say we go and find Mary," Walt said, and he was tighter than a fiddle string.

"That would be a good idea." I snapped open the breach and inserted a fresh round into the chamber. "Now you boys stay put," I said, turning to the crowd and giving Walt a nod.

He skipped up the street to the corner. I followed, keeping the company of men at the Glory Hole Saloon in my sight.

Walt was waiting for me around the corner. "Which way?"

I pointed at an alley halfway down the street. We hurried into the deeper shadows and paused to reconnoiter. "They'll be after us in a few minutes," I said. "Soon as they get their nerve up and their guns ready."

"We can't fight the whole town, Abernathy."

"Have any suggestions?"

He thought a moment and then shook his head. "No, none other than hightailing out of here while we still have a chance."

"On foot?"

"Guess we wouldn't get far."

"And it still will leave Mary," I said. Two men hurried past the mouth of the alley. When they had gone I nodded and we made our way around garbage cans and past a hidden creature with shiny green eyes that watched our stalking passage out.

The alley deposited us upon a deserted street the next block over. As far as I could tell, the "friends" had not yet mustered sufficient numbers to mount an attack. It was only a matter of time. They would have to find us, of course, but Lacy Springs wasn't so large a town that they would have any problems in that department.

Walt said, "We ain't never gonna find her this way. They might be on their way down to the States right now."

We moved down the street, sticking close to the shadowed side, away from the business district, and entered what little residential area there was. Beyond the dark roofs the silhouette of the church stood against a drifting pattern of moonlit clouds. I stopped and studied a movement down the street.

"What is it?" he asked.

"That's the wagon Cary drove away in, and the horses are still hitched up." It was pulled up alongside a house. There was a light behind the drawn curtains.

In the distance came the growing sounds of an angry mob. I motioned Walt to follow. I checked out horses and wagon, certain it was the same rig that had skittered around the corner a second before I'd squared my sights on the driver's back. We sidled up against the building and made our way to the back door. It was locked. The sounds of men in the street grew louder. We edged up the side where a curtained window glowed from a lamp burning inside.

"See anything?" Walt asked.

"No."

A shadow passed across the curtain.

We backed away from the window and hunkered down. I said, "We need to get him to open up. He has never seen you, so you might try knocking on the front door."

"He'll be suspicious, and what'll I say if it isn't him in there?"

"I don't know. Be creative. Ask him for directions or something. Act surprised and tell him you got the wrong house."

"And where will you be?"

"Right beside you."

Walt climbed the single step to a porch, looked back, and waited as I positioned myself in the shadows that grew up beside the door.

He knocked.

"Who's that?" came Cary's voice from the other side of the door.

Walt gave me a questioning glance. "Make up a name," I said softly from the bushes.

Walt cleared his throat and said, "I'm looking for Virgil Collins."

"Ain't nobody by that name here," Cary said.

"Keep him talking," I whispered.

"I was told I could find him at this house."

"You was told wrong, now get moving."

"Can you tell me where he might be found?"

This wasn't going to get the door opened. I stepped out from the bushes and hurried around back to the locked door. There was a slight play in the locking mechanism that allowed the door to rattle back and forth a quarter inch. I set the rifle against the wall, stepped back, and threw myself into the door. The lock wasn't much of a lock, and it took out a section of door frame with it as I crashed into the room.

I'd landed in darkness. A door, outlined with the light coming from the next room, was set into one wall. By now Cary knew what was happening. I touched the door handle, turned it, and immediately withdrew my hand. A pistol shot three times and three splintered holes appeared in the door allowing more light to stream into the darkness.

I burst through, flattening onto the floor, and put Cary in my sights. He whirled around and the next instant Mary was lined up with the front blade of my pistol. I sucked in a breath and moved my finger away from the trigger. Cary's face peered down at me from over her shoulder. His gun pointed at me while his left arm pulled her firmly in front of him.

"Don't try nothing, Gate," he said, waving the gun nervously.

"Abernathy!" Mary said.

"Let her go, Cary."

He poked the barrel of his pistol into Mary's side. "I ain't takin' no chances with you, Able Gate," he said.

Out front, Walt banged on the door again. Cary glanced at it then said, "Tell whoever is out there to go away."

Mary winced as the gun dug deeper into her side.

"Tell him, Gate, or she's dead."

"Walt," I said.

"You okay, Abernathy?"

"So far."

"Open the door."

"I can't, not yet. He wants you to leave. Maybe it will be better if you do. He has a gun on Mary."

"All right, I'm backing off. But there are some people coming up the street and I think they're friends of McClain's."

Cary shifted on the balls of his feet. "Okay, Gate, now you drop your gun."

"Gate?" Mary said, confused. She seemed to have a fairly good grip on herself.

Cary's fingers whitened around the pistol. "I said drop it!"

The kid seemed more scared than Mary. I said, "You're the one that had better drop your gun. Think about it. You shoot her, you've lost your cover. You shoot me, you better make sure you kill me with the first shot because I won't worry about who is in my way at that point." I gambled he was scared enough not to see through that lie. I said, "If you stop now you have a good chance of walking out of here. Otherwise you have no chance at all." It was bold talk, and almost anyone could have seen I was bluffing, but Cary was scared, and he wasn't thinking straight, and either that could work for me or it could drive him to do something crazy.

"You wouldn't," he said.

Mary's expression told me she wasn't sure I wouldn't either. Too many contradictory items were assaulting her nice, logical world at once. Nice people don't kidnap you. Nice people don't stick guns in your ribs. Nice people don't tell you their name is Abernathy Gatelatch when it really is Able Gate. Maybe a person who'd do that really would shoot you to get at the man standing behind you.

"You wouldn't shoot her," he said more confidently.

"Try me."

The look in his eyes made me go cold. He was weighing the chances. One part of my brain was making plans for my next move while another, more distant portion was calculating how many men were now coming up the street, how close they were, and how many more guns I'd have to face before we were out of here.

The window behind him shattered. A piece of wood came flying through, ripping down the curtains, and Cary whirled toward the sound. I sprang for the gun in his hand, wrenching it up and away. It fired once into the ceiling before I knocked it to the floor. Mary pushed herself away from us and I swung a fist into Cary's gut. The wind went out of him and he fell back onto his rump and sat there bent over, hugging himself.

Walt was clearing the jagged window glass with his pistol. He stepped through and stood there looking at me. "Is he shot?"

"No," I said, gathering up my gun and Cary's. I stepped toward Mary and she backed away. "You all right?"

She nodded her head. "Yes."

Walt said, "We better get the hell out of here, Abernathy…begging your pardon Mary. There's a bunch of angry people gathering out front."

I took her hand. She stiffened at first then came along.

"What about him?" Walt asked.

"Let him be."

"If you say so."

"Out the back door," I said, and paused to look back at Cary kneeling there, wishing, for a moment, that I had a pebble to toss at him. I dismissed the idea as being vindictive and childish—but it sure as hell would have been satisfying.

Able Gate

23

THE CLAMOR OF MEN out front was making a loud noise in back as we hurried out the door. I snatched up the Springfield I'd left there while Walt turned his head side to side as if in a daze.

"We can't go that way," he said, glancing toward the front of the house.

"Like hell we can't." I hoisted Mary onto the buggy seat and Walt leaped over the sideboard. I kicked off the brake, giving the reins a violent snap.

We lurched forward. At the front of the house men scattered aside like so many clucking chickens on a country road. Gunfire erupted at our backs. Walt returned fire as I whipped the reins and shoved Mary's head down between her knees. The buggy slipped sideways out onto the street, righted itself and took off, horses responding to the reins, my yelling, and the harsh bark of Walt's pistol behind them.

Splintering wood ripped from the buggy and the gunfire behind us grew and merged into a Gatling gun-like cacophony. We swung out onto the main street, about to disappear around the corner, when one of the horses stumbled. It regained its footing, took three more strides, then stumbled again, sinking to its knees. The buggy reeled sideways.

Mary and I flew clear as the buggy flipped once and ground to a halt. Walt leaped at the last moment and landed a few feet from the overturned wreckage.

"You okay?" he asked, hurrying over to where we had landed in the street.

Mary nodded her head, dazed. I helped her to her feet and pulled my rifle free of the twisted pieces of wood. The one horse was struggling to its feet against the dead weight of its companion.

"What now?" Mary said, regaining her balance.

"Over there!" We ran up to the locked door of Grumbly's Mining Supplies and Tools. I put a bullet through the lock and kicked the door open. Inside, the night grew blacker as I rammed the door shut. Walt helped me roll a heavy keg that must have contained sand or gravel in front of the door, and then we scrambled down behind some unrecognizable machinery covered with a tarp to regroup.

"That was close," Walt said.

"It's not over yet," I said, glancing around the murky interior of the warehouse as my eyes slowly adjusted.

Mary was watching me and when I looked at her she said, "You wouldn't really have…?"

I grinned. "What do you think?"

She let go of the breath that had caught up inside her and said, "I didn't think so, but…" She hesitated. "You really are Able Gate?"

"You make it sound like a disease."

"I didn't mean it that way, only, well, why didn't you tell us?"

"I couldn't."

She didn't understand and I didn't feel like I could take the time now to explain the thinking processes of military men like Colonel Rundles—or myself, for that matter. "Gate!"

The voice pulled my eyes from her. It was a voice I recognized from the sidewalk in front of the saloon. "We've got you surrounded and you'll have to come out sooner or later. We've taken away your horses."

Walt squirmed and said, "He's right. There's no way we're gonna get out of here, Abernathy!"

"Is that true?" Mary asked, and in the darkness her eyes widened, their deep blue color lost in the shadows that softly contoured her face. The darkness added an air of mystery to her, something not apparent in the revealing light of day. It would make an interesting study in black and white…someday.

I said to Walt, "Keep your gun on that door and if anything comes through it shoot it."

"Where are you going?"

"I want to check out something. I'll be moving around in the dark back here so try not to get too nervous with that gun." I turned to Mary. "Do you know how to use one of these?"

Her shoulders raised in a shrug and she said, "A little. I know how to shoot them but I'm not too certain I can hit anything with one."

I reloaded Cary's revolver, lowering the hammer on an empty chamber. "You've got five shots left in that one. If you have to use it, wait until your target is almost on top of you. At ten feet you should be able to hit a man with your eyes closed."

"I wouldn't close my eyes, Mr. Gate," she came back sharply, and I grinned into the darkness as I left them there. Anger was a great stimulant, and it wouldn't do Mary any harm now.

The high, dingy windows overhead were only slightly brighter than the huge belly of the warehouse. I felt a certain kinship with Jonah as I worked my way through the narrow

155

passageways of wooden crates and hulking, canvas covered machinery. At a suspicious-looking box I paused, bent to read the label, and then as a last resort struck a match. In the flaring light appeared the words DRILL BITS. I could think of no good use for drill bits, except as clubs when bullets ran out. The fire ate its way down the stick as I looked around seeing only more crates and tarps.

The flame kissed my fingertip and I ground it out under the toe of my boot. At the back of the building I stopped in front of an iron door set into the wall. A single piece of bent metal rod stuck through the latch where a padlock ought to have been to keep it closed. Simple enough. The heavy door squealed as I hauled it back.

It was blacker than sin inside the vault. I felt inside my vest pocket for another match, but there were no more. They had all gone into the fire, and Carl and Weevil had gone to their graves—and now here was Cary, in a town in a country where neither one of us would have guessed five days ago we'd be meeting again.

"Gate! Able Gate! Show yourself so's we can talk."

"Like hell," I said to myself, thinking of the red-bearded man who had promised to carry me out of town in the back of a wagon. I turned back inside the vault to discover a wall of boxes an arm's length in front of me. I pulled one off into my arms pretty sure from the heft of it that I had found what I was looking for.

I stopped on my way back up front to eye the big, sliding freight doors on the south wall of the building. A stout padlock secured them on the inside. No one would be coming in from that quarter.

"What do you have there?" Walt asked when I pushed the box safely behind the metal boiler plates of a small steam engine.

"Reinforcements."

He looked at me curiously as I opened the box.

"Dynamite!" he exclaimed.

156

"Is it dangerous?" Mary asked, inching closer.

"Yes, ma'am," I said.

She withdrew.

"But only if struck by a bullet or armed with a blasting cap. As they are now, they couldn't hurt a fly." I glanced at Walt. "Anything happen while I was gone?"

"Someone rattled the door handle but thought better of trying to come through it."

"They won't try anything till daylight," I said, opening my watch and turning it to the windows high overhead. "And that won't be for another six hours."

"What do we do till then?" Mary asked, eyeing the box of dynamite.

"I'm open to suggestions."

"We can sneak out of here," Walt said.

"There are two doors, maybe a third one someplace, but I didn't see it. We won't get very far going out the front door, not with a townful of guns waiting out there, and the side door is secured with a padlock."

Walt sat against the boiler to think.

"I'm hungry," Mary said after a while.

I wasn't surprised. Cary and his kin had not been big on hospitality where food was concerned.

The blackness against the windows faded to gray as the dawn neared, and with the approaching light footsteps began to tap across the roof. Beyond a window next to the door, scurrying shadows warned that something was afoot. Throughout the early part of the night, the man with the red beard had called out regularly, but that had stopped some hours ago. Now it began again.

"Gate!"

"He must have crawled out of bed," Walt said softly at my side.

"It's comforting to know he's well rested," I said, then aloud: "What do you want?"

He stepped off the sidewalk across the street and came out into the street. With a brightening sky behind him, he stopped twenty feet off and put his hands on his hips, his right one close to the grip of a pistol.

"Sleep well?" the man asked.

"Bastard," I whispered, and Walt managed to find a grin somewhere among his apprehensions. "Like a baby," I said.

"You ready to come out so's we can talk about it?"

Mary came hurrying forward. She dropped to one knee below the window and said, "There is a third door, Abernathy. It's back in that corner." She was waving the gun around and pointing with it.

I moved the barrel away from my chest. "Sorry," she said, pointing the muzzle down at the floor.

"Is it locked?"

"I don't know. Maybe from the outside. I didn't try it. I suppose I should of."

"You folks must be getting pretty hungry in there. Come on out and we'll talk this over over breakfast. I'm buying."

"Does he mean that?" Mary asked.

"Sure he does," I said, "and he probably has some choice real estate on downtown Regina he'd be willing to sell you real cheap too."

She looked at me sharply. "I think I liked you better as Abernathy Gatelatch."

"Sorry."

She smiled thinly. "I guess we're all feeling the strain."

I said to Walt, "Go with Mary and check out that door. Maybe push something heavy in front of it to slow them down."

He and Mary moved away.

The man out front waited in the growing light. "Well?" he said after a few moments.

"I think we'll pass," I called out. My reply was immediately answered by the crack of a rifle. Glass shattered into the warehouse.

Overhead, a rectangle of light opened in the ceiling. A face appeared, and then a hand holding a gun. I swung around and fired through the ceiling where I calculated the rest of the man would be found. The gun fell onto a stretched tarp and someone hauled the body from the opening.

At the back of the warehouse a gun fired twice. In the street the red-bearded man dove for cover. Then gunfire seemed to explode all at once from every direction. I crawled down behind some heavy iron machinery as splinters ripped inward from the wooden walls all around.

Another face appeared at the trapdoor in the ceiling and I fired at it. I don't know if I hit him or not, but as the smoke cleared the rectangle of brightening morning sky in the ceiling was empty, and it stayed that way.

With morning crowding the shadows out, I was able to see the trapdoor clearly, and the catwalk that ran below it. A coil of rope was draped over the railing and a wooden keg that might have contained roofing nails sat on the catwalk off to one side.

From the back of the warehouse came a crash that sounded like half the building had caved in on itself. A moment later Walt and Mary were hurrying up an aisle of machinery like soldiers behind a low barricade.

"What was all that about?"

"They tried coming through," Walt said, glancing back over his shoulder. "A couple of bullets warned them back. Then Mary and me, we heaved a tall shelf of machine parts over onto the door. It closed that opening down solid." He grinned.

I pointed up at the ceiling. "We've got another opening to contend with."

"Oh, no." Despair had worked its way into Mary's voice.

"It could work in our favor," I said.

"How's that?" Walt asked.

"Think you can find a way up there?"

He surveyed the length of the catwalk and his eyes came to rest on the top portion of a two-by-four ladder nailed up against the back wall.

"Reckon I could," he said.

I opened our cache of dynamite. "Stuff your pockets."

"What am I suppose to do with them?"

"How good are you at throwing?"

He shrugged his shoulders and then the confusion left his face, pushed aside by a spreading grin of understanding. "How good really are you with that gun, Gate?"

"Let's find out."

24

THE THICK, red-wrapped sticks were bound in clusters of threes. Walt managed to find room for nearly a dozen of them in various pockets.

"Try not to get hit." I grinned.

"Thanks. The Fourth of July would make a mighty poor showing, wouldn't it?" He moved off toward the back of the warehouse.

"Gate!" Red Beard said, and the gunfire tapered off. "You still alive in there?"

"We're doing just fine." I inched up to the glassless window frame. "But you boys are sure playing hell with this building. Hope you got the owner's permission to shoot his place up like you are."

"He was a friend of Barrister's too."

"McClain seemed to of had a lot of friends in town."

"He was good for business," Red Beard said. "Always brought in lots of new money and was real free with the way he spent it. Helped a lot of folks out of hard times."

It didn't sound like the Barrister McClain I knew, but then, buying a safe harbor made a lot of sense. I had done the same thing. It had cost McClain money that wasn't his own; had cost me a name and reputation that weren't my own. It wasn't exactly the most comfortable comparison I had ever made, and I reminded myself that there really was no similarity between McClain and myself, after all.

I said, "That money was stolen, and its owners murdered."

"Life is tough all over, Gate. We all have our own problems. Breakfast is still on if you're interested."

Walt had worked his way up the ladder, his pockets bulging. I checked my watch again, and now that the thunder of gunfire had died away I listened for any faraway sounds. Hearing nothing but the creak of boards as Walt made his way across the catwalk, I turned my attention back to the man in the street.

"What's your name, mister?"

"Boyton. Boyton Davenport."

"Well, Mr. Boyton Davenport, we do appreciate the offer, but I think for the time being we'll just stay low...unless you can come up with a spicier deal than breakfast."

Walt poked his head through the trapdoor. "No one up here," he called down.

I holstered my pistol and checked the Springfield. Closing the breech on a live round, I nodded my head at him.

Boyton said, "Have it your way, Gate. We're in no hurry out here. We got plenty of time and plenty of bullets. Think about that. We can make it mighty hot in there for you and your friends."

Mary eyed me like a mouse backed into a corner by a cat. "I hope you know what you're doing, Abernathy," she said.

"You're not the only one," I said. "You hear anything?"

She paused a moment, temporarily siderailed by my question. "No," she said. "What am I suppose to be listening for?"

"Train whistles."

Walt stood out of the trapdoor and heaved back. I called out to Boyton, "It should start getting pretty hot for you out there too."

"What do you mean, Gate?"

In the brightening sky a red bundle sailed through the air. I snapped the Springfield up and caught it in my sights as it hit the ground by a building across the street and bounced once. Boyton dove aside at the sight of my rifle pointing out the window, but it wasn't him I was aiming at.

I squeezed the trigger and the rifle punched me soundly in the shoulder. Thunder sounded and the ground erupted, throwing out a shower of dirt and sticks. The corner of the porch across the way sagged then caved in. Men scurried away from the groaning wood like survivors from a sinking ship.

"Give 'em another!" I shouted up to Walt.

The bundle of sticks tumbled through the air. I lined up with them and touched the trigger. The concussion of detonating dynamite a dozen feet above the ground knocked men to their knees and burst windows.

"How was that?" Walt called down.

His words sounded far away through the ringing in my ears.

"Try to get the next one farther," I called back. Gunfire had started up again along the street, but in the confusion and settling dust I could not pinpoint its location.

Walt reared back and let go of another bundle almost before I had fed a fresh round into the rifle. It bounced on the roof across the street, and I caught it as it began to roll toward the gutter. Shingle and timber shrapnel went flying.

On her knees by the steam engine, Mary plugged her ears and clenched her teeth. The pistol resided in her lap. I could feel her tension rise as I followed the arc of a forth bundle of TNT and squeezed the trigger. A plume of brown dust momentarily obscured the street and slowly drifted on the morning wind toward the twisted wreckage that only a minute before had been a perfectly functional building.

I missed the fifth bundle altogether. It bounced once in the middle of the street and was immediately blanketed by a passing wall of dust. Then the Springfield jammed. I slammed the breech again with the palm of my hand and ripped off the rim of the cartridge, but the casing stayed stubbornly wedged inside the chamber.

"What's the matter?" Walt yelled down at me.

"Cartridge stuck," I said, opening the blade of my pocketknife.

The gunfire picked up again and wood splinters ripped from the wall at various angles, stinging my cheek.

"I'm coming down to help."

"No. I'll get it in a second...wait! I have an idea." I snapped open the lid of my watch, then shoved it back into my pocket. "Can you throw a rope around that keg and lower it down?"

Walt opened the lid. "It's full of nails."

"That's what I figured. Think you can get it down?"

He tipped it to one side experimentally and said that it wasn't too heavy and that he thought he could. He lifted the coil of rope from the railing and threaded it through a pair of holes on the rim of the keg.

The gunfire stopped again and Red Beard's voice boomed across the sudden silence. "Gate? Able Gate?"

Mary looked at me.

"Let him wonder," I said softly. "Keep an eye on that window. I'm gonna give Walt a hand."

"Abernathy...I mean...Able?"

"Abernathy is just fine."

"But you're not Abernathy Gatelatch."

"A part of me is," I said, comprehending her confusion and the dilemma that confronted her. Who was I, really? Who was the man she had found an interest in? Was it the same man who would have escorted her to the Armory Dance?

"And a part of you is Able Gate," she said with cool detachment.

"Does it make a difference?"

Mary started to say something, stopped and shook her head. "I don't know."

"We'll have time to talk about it later."

"Will we?" The coolness was gone, giving way to a flood of emotions she was fighting desperately to keep from coming out.

I grinned at her, hoping my confidence would help her— help me also, to believe that we three would leave this place alive. I checked my watch again and said, "If the CPR keeps to any kind of reasonable schedule, we'll be out of here in no time."

"Gate! You need some help in there?" Red Beard said.

"Keep an eye on the window," I reminded her softly, touched her hand, then moved off to help Walt with the nail keg.

Walt nudged the keg over the edge of the catwalk with the toe of his boot. His shoulders bunched as they took the full weight of it, hand over handing it down to me. I wrapped my arms about the keg when it came within reach and eased it to the floor. He lashed the end of the rope and slid down. "What do you have in mind?"

"Help me get this over by the door."

"Gate?"

"You're being summoned," Walt said.

"Let Red Beard wonder a bit longer."

Walt looked out the window and whistled softly. "We did all that?"

"The best is yet to come." I pried the cover off the keg. It was more than three-quarters full of nails, which left plenty of room. "What do you mean?"

"Hey! You folks needing a doctor in there yet? Gate, if you can still hear me just call out. I'm still buying breakfast if'n you got a mind to eat. After all that shooting you people must be getting right hungry." Red Beard approached the warehouse with caution and stopped a dozen feet from the ramp that angled down from the door.

"How much dynamite do you have left?"

"Three bundles."

"Let me have them."

Walt pulled dynamite from various pockets and handed them over. "Hoooly shit!" he said when I began carefully packing the explosive into the top of the keg. "Pardon me, ma'am." He glanced quickly at Mary but she hadn't heard him. Her concentration was directed at the bundles of dynamite I was packing in among the nails.

"I can fit more in here," I said.

Walt crawled off and came back with two more red bundles.

"Is that safe?" Mary asked as I hammered the top back in place with the butt of my pistol.

"Depends."

She blinked and seemed to come out of her trance. "Depends on what?"

"On how close you happen to be to it when it goes off."

"Humor is not appreciated at the moment, thank you, Mr. Gate."

"I can't think of a time it's not needed more," Walt said.

She pretended she didn't hear his comment and began to speak when she suddenly stopped and cocked her head. "I hear it!"

Walt and I looked at her.

"There!" she said, pointing toward the rear of the warehouse.

"What?"

I waved a hand at him to be silent and listened. My ears rang from the tumult of the gunfire, but even with a swarm of bees inside my head, I heard it too, the distant shrill of a train whistle, growing louder.

"It's too early," I said, tipping the keg on its side and rolling it toward the barricaded door.

Able Gate

25

"I DON'T UNDERSTAND," Mary said, and from the look on his face, neither did Walt.

I said, "Hand me my rifle," and resumed working at the jammed shell with my pocketknife. "The way I figure it, there is no way we are going to shoot our way out of this spot, and if we did, how far could we get on foot?"

"We're going to hop a train," Mary said suddenly.

"According to the schedule posted on the depot window that I saw last night, at seven-ten this morning there's a freighter due through here. It's not scheduled to stop but generally when one comes through a town it slows up."

"We still have to get to it," Walt said. "Right out that side door is a loading dock, and beyond that two flatcars sitting on the siding. The main line isn't more than five feet beyond."

"That door is locked. You said so yourself."

"You have a gun, don't you?"

"They'll figure out what's going on."

"They aren't going to have time to think about it." I patted the nail keg lovingly where it lay upon its side in front of the door.

Walt thought it over and said, "Your timing is going to have to be almost perfect."

"We're running a gamble, I admit. If either of you has a better plan, this is the time to tell."

"It's worth a try," Mary said.

The train whistle sounded again, two shorts and a long. I said, "We haven't enough time to figure the odds. Just cross your fingers and hope there's an empty flatcar or open boxcar on that train."

"Yes, there's that too," Walt said.

Out in the street Red Beard said, "I see you're not interested in talking, Gate. Maybe if we warm the place up a bit more you'll change your mind."

"Get ready, we haven't any time to waste," I said.

Walt and Mary went to the side doors and Walt pointed his pistol at the lock then looked over at me. I worked the jammed shell from the Springfield and slid in a fresh one, closing the breech on it.

Moving up to the hole in the wall where the window had once resided, I called out to Red Beard. "I think we're ready for that breakfast, if the offer is still on."

Red Beard's smile widened; lips showed through the forest of red hair on his face. I shouldered aside the barricade in front of the door and slipped the bolt.

"The offer is still good, Gate. Come on out, we'll hold our fire."

"Like hell you will," I said softly, and then aloud: "All right, we're coming out now." I pushed the door open and hung back in the shadows. I raised the rifle to my shoulder and brought the front sight down on the lonely red bundle of dynamite in the middle of the street while behind me the whistle of the approaching freighter sounded as if it were nearly atop us.

Red Beard figured something was wrong after about ten seconds and we didn't show.

"What are you trying to pull, Gate?" he said, and I touched the trigger. An invisible fist knocked Red Beard to the ground and a plume of brown dust climbed up from a new hole in the middle of the street. The explosion muffled the sound of the train as it came into town from the north. Behind me, Walt's pistol made a much smaller noise. A rectangle of light opened up, making me visible to those out in front. Ramming home a fresh shell, I propped my foot upon the keg and gave it a shove. It wobbled out the door like a drunken soldier on a Saturday night and then it started down the ramp, gaining speed as it raced out into the middle of the pockmarked street.

Gunfire poured into the building. I tried not to think of that, or of the wooden walls that were splintering to pieces in front of my eyes. I cleared my mind of all thoughts but lining up on that wobbling barrel. The hammer dropped and the rifle bucked against my shoulder.

Every shred of glass that still remained in the warehouse instantly vaporized. My eardrums exploded and the world went black around me.

When I opened my eyes again I was lying on my back behind the little steam engine. The tarp that had covered it was in shreds. Something warm was running into my eyes and something impatient was tugging at my arm.

"Get up, Able! Get up!"

I recognized Walt's voice. It was urgent; too urgent to wait until the world stopped doing circus tricks. The whistle of an approaching train shrilled powerfully, as if the locomotive were about to run over us.

My feet came up under me and I shook my head to clear my vision. A glance out the ragged hole in the wall of the warehouse caused me to pause and suck in a quick breath. Nothing moved but the massive brown cloud that had begun to shift and swirl on the morning breeze like an apparition out

171

of a Dickens novel. Through the tendrils of brown dust the
shattered remains of the buildings across the street took form.
Doll-like shapes lay about, strangely red, and contorted as if
stuffed with eiderdown. Walt was tugging my arm. I turned
away from the bloody scene only to see Mary standing wide-
eyed at the gaping side doors.

"Hurry up!" she was saying. I more read the words on her
lips and in her frantic arm movements than actually heard
them.

There was a train passing outside. Its shadow flickered
against the tarp-covered shape that stood out sharply now in
the morning sunlight. Suddenly the world I once knew
returned vividly to me. I remembered the staccato gunfire, the
bullets ripping apart the warehouse walls, the keg of nails
with its deadly cargo. I remember lining up my sights on it
and squeezing the trigger oh so gently even as a dozen guns
spit lead and death into the building...and I remembered
something else too.

The train!

My brain cleared. I leaped ahead of Walt, taking Mary by
the hand, and stepped into the sunlight. The boxcars swayed
before us, morning sunlight flickering between them like
blinding bursts from a photographer's flash. We jumped to
the parked flatcars—close enough to feel the wind of the
passing train upon our faces. I looked down the long line of
cars and spied one with its door open. As it approached I took
Mary by her waist and at the right moment lifted her and
heaved her through the passing door.

"You take the next one," I yelled over the clatter of iron
wheels upon iron rails.

Walt nodded and stuck out his hand. For a moment I
thought he wanted to shake but he was only handing me my
rifle.

"Thanks," I said, and then an open door presented itself
and Walt leaped through.

The end of the train was fast approaching and no more open doors waited for me. I slung the rifle over my shoulder, clenched my teeth, and aimed at the iron-rung ladder of the caboose. I made some mental ciphers, pictured a battered, iron skillet, led it slightly...and leaped.

26

COLONEL OLIVER RUNDLES looked particularly unhappy. His brooding eyes moved from Walt to Mary Landers and finally settled heavily on me. I had the distinct feeling he would have preferred I'd come back alone although he would never have admitted that, publicly or even in private.

"Then this man, Cary, is still alive," he said when I'd finished relating the events of the last three days.

"He is."

"Unfortunate." Rundles's expression went blank and he reached for the cigar box he always kept on the corner of his desk. The painted rock was back in its place too, holding down a stack of unruly papers on the left-hand side of the desk. The crystal pitcher had returned home to the silver set and his revolver had found its way back into the U.S. Cavalry holster that hung from a peg in the wall next to the big map behind his chair. Everything was as it should be—or so it appeared.

"Then we might prepare ourselves for trouble from that quarter," he said, snipping the end from a cigar and sticking it into a corner of his mouth. He remembered his manners and offered Walt and me a cigar from the box.

Walt accepted. I said no thanks.

"Too early?"

"Not before I've eaten," I said.

"Oh, yes. I've forgotten." He looked at Mary and said, "You must be starved, my dear."

"Yes. I am rather hungry."

"I expect your parents to be along shortly," he said, passing a match around. "I sent a man out to collect them for you. You'll be anxious to get home."

"Yes," Mary said with a heavy weariness that reflected how each of us felt.

I said, "I rather doubt we will have any trouble from Cary, sir. The last I saw of him, he seemed anxious to see as much distance put between us as possible."

Rundles grunted. "Perhaps not him personally. But the information he carries may nevertheless fall into other hands. We may yet see it come back to haunt us." He glanced at Walt and Mary, cleared his throat, and said, "Well, we can discuss the ramifications of this another time."

There was a knock at the door. "Come in," Rundles said.

Lundt appeared against a backdrop of the parade ground, a column of marching recruits and the colonel's carriage just visible behind him. Mary's mother and father rushed inside and engulfed their daughter with hugs and tears. Walt and I each had our fists crushed by a joyous father.

"We can't thank you enough," her father said to the three of us and to no one of us in particular.

Rundles accepted the thank you for all of us and advised they take Mary home and feed her and tuck her into bed. He got his fist crushed and pumped and his cheek kissed. As they took Mary down to the waiting carriage, she glanced back at Walt and me with a look on her face that I could not read. Then she stepped up into the carriage and they were all whisked away by Private Frederick Lundt aboard the front seat.

Rundles's eyes were scrutinizing me when I looked back. He sat down in his chair and said to Walt, "You might as well go on home too. If I have any other questions I'll send someone out to find you."

"Yeah, sure," he said, glancing at me and wrinkling the brim of his hat in his fingers. "Well, I guess I'll see you around, Abernathy."

"See you around, Walt," I said.

"Ah—I, I just want to let you know that your secret is safe with me," he said, and glanced at Rundles who gave him a thin smile in return.

"Thanks, Walt."

He nodded his head, casting a brief look at Rundles one more time to be sure it was really all right to leave. He stuck the cigar back into his mouth and scuffed out, shutting the door behind him.

"Well, Abe," Rundles said after a few quiet moments of contemplating the blue-gray haze that had taken shape above his desk. He flicked a cylinder of ash toward the urn, missed it, and said, "What are we going to do about you now?"

"That shouldn't be a problem, sir," I said, settling in the chair before his desk.

"Oh?" His eyebrows hitched up a fraction and those cold eyes bore holes into mine.

I said, "I'm resigning."

The cigar tipped from his lips. "You're what?"

"Resigning. Mustering out. Call it what you will. I'm leaving."

"But you can't."

"My tour is up in three months, and when it is I don't intend to reenlist."

"Now, let's not do anything rash," he said. "I'm not. I've thought it through and decided I've given the cavalry a good portion of my life. I want the rest of it for myself." Rundles squirmed in his seat a bit before straightening up and regaining his aura of authority. "It's your decision, of course. Is there anything I can say or do that will change your mind?"

I shrugged my shoulders. "Nothing is carved in granite, but at the moment I can't think of anything you could offer me to change my mind."

That seemed to satisfy him. His lips came together thoughtfully and then a small smile surfaced. "Well, I have three months to work on it, then."

I stood up. "That you have. Anything else you want to talk to me about, Ollie?"

He shook his head. "Not at the present."

"Then I'll be going too."

"What are your plans?"

"Immediate or long range?"

"Immediate," he said, and pulled heavily on the cigar.

"I'm going to see how Tippi is doing," I said, dropping my hat upon my head. "I asked Randy about her on the way back, but he didn't know any more than I. Apparently he left shortly after I had and had been incommunicado, riding in circles along the Canadian border until he saw us waving at him from the open door of a Canadian and Pacific Railroad box car."

Something changed in Rundles's eyes. "That reminds me," he said, pulling open the top drawer of his desk and setting the three pouches of gold atop the cigar box. "You wanted me to keep these for you. I believe your intention was for me to give them to Sara Ann in the event you did not return."

I'd forgotten them. I reached for the pouches, smiling, and said, "Fortunately, I can give them to her myself." My hand stopped midway and I looked at him sharply. He was grinning.

"Sara Ann?" I said.

"Yes, Sara Ann. Tippi's daughter. She has been with Tippi constantly for the last two days, and according to Doc

178

Bidley, Tippi is making a remarkable recovery. Doc can't stop talking about it. You know Doc. When he can't stop talking about a thing it's certainly good."

I grinned. "So she told Tippi who she was."

"And you knew all along." He frowned. "After this, I don't want to hear another word about half-truths and unspoken lies, Abe." He flourished the wrinkled letter I had returned to him, then ripped it into quarters, and the quarters into quarters, dropping the pieces into his wastebasket. "I think both Tippi and Sara will be quite pleased to see you. That expectant mother has been worrying herself sick about you ever since you left. You have no right to do that to a woman in her condition."

"Yes, sir," I said, throwing him a mock salute. I turned for the door.

"Oh, Abe."

I looked back. Rundles was puffing contentedly on the cigar, which he held between the stub of two missing fingertips. "I'd appreciate it if you left the gun."

I dropped the holster on his desk. "Kind of late for this, isn't it, Ollie?" I reminded him.

"Perhaps, but I still have three months, and I'm still in command."

"For three months," I said.

I left him sitting there, puffing on his cigar, and there was a strange gleam in his eyes: the cool, calculating look of a tactician planning to move into battle. I had a feeling these next three months might prove to be the toughest challenge I'd ever have to face.

A look at Mississippi Pirates, by Douglas Hirt

In the golden age of the Mississippi, the river was a path that led to freedom, opportunity, and danger. Captain William Hamilton's Tempest Queen was his life, and he would let no one take that from him. On board were the beautiful Miss Cora Mills, the kind of lady men fought over; Lt. Sherman Dempsey, delivering gold to Fort Leavenworth; and "Reverend" Saunders - a scheming river pirate.

Available from Wolfpack Publishing and Douglas Hirt.

About the Author

Douglas Hirt was born in Illinois, but heeding Horace Greeley's admonition to "Go west, young man", he headed to New Mexico at eighteen. Doug earned a Bachelor's degree from the College of Santa Fe and a Masters of Science degree from Eastern New Mexico University. During this time he spent several summers living in a tent in the desert near Carlsbad, New Mexico, conducting biological baseline surveys for the Department of Energy.

Doug drew heavily from this "desert life" when writing his first novel, DEVIL'S WIND. In 1991 Doug's novel, A PASSAGE OF SEASONS, won the Colorado Authors' League Top Hand Award. His 1998 book, BRANDISH, and 1999 DEADWOOD, were finalists for the SPUR award given by the Western Writers of America.

A short story writer, and the author of twenty-nine novels and one book of non fiction, Doug now makes his home in Colorado Springs with his wife Kathy and their two children, Rebecca and Derick. When not writing or traveling to research his novels, Doug enjoys collecting and restoring old English sports cars.

Discover more great titles by Douglas Hirt and Wolfpack Publishing at:
http://wolfpackpublishing.com/douglas-hirt/

Able Gate

1481168
Western Hirt

$6.99

67403363R00105

Made in the USA
Lexington, KY
10 September 2017